We hope you enjoy this book.
Please return or renew it by the due date.
You can renew it at **www.norfolk.gov.uk/libraries**
or by using our free library app. Otherwise you can
phone **0344 800 8020** - please have your library
card and pin ready.
You can sign up for email reminders too.

16 10 19		

NORFOLK COUNTY COUNCIL
LIBRARY AND INFORMATION SERVICE

NORFOLK ITEM

Also by Robert J. Steelman and available from Center Point Large Print:

The Fox Dancer
Sun Boy

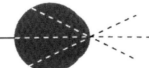

**This Large Print Book carries the
Seal of Approval of N.A.V.H.**

CHEYENNE VENGEANCE

Robert J. Steelman

CENTER POINT LARGE PRINT
THORNDIKE, MAINE

This Center Point Large Print edition
is published in the year 2018 by arrangement with
Golden West Literary Agency.

First US edition: Doubleday

The text of this Large Print edition is unabridged.
In other aspects, this book may vary
from the original edition.

Set in 16-point Times New Roman type.

ISBN: 978-1-68324-999-3 (hardcover)
ISBN: 978-1-64358-003-6 (paperback)

Library of Congress Cataloging-in-Publication Data

Names: Steelman, Robert J., author.
Title: Cheyenne vengeance / Robert J. Steelman.
Description: Center Point Large Print edition. | Thorndike, Maine :
    Center Point Large Print, 2018.
Identifiers: LCCN 2018038603| ISBN 9781683249993
    (hardcover : a   alk. paper)
Subjects: LCSH
Classification: L(3/.54—dc23
LC record availa

Printed and
by TJ International Ltd, Padstow, Cornwall

MIX
Paper from
responsible sources
FSC® C013056

CHAPTER ONE

It was the time we Cheyennes call *Makikomini*, the Big Hard-Face Moon. The whites called it December; all round Fort McPherson they were getting ready for a feast named Christmas. Neither my friend Kingfisher nor I understood what it was about. Reverend Parsley tried to explain, but it didn't make much sense.

When we orphan boys were not in classes at the Indian Salvation School, we were supposed to pick up papers and trash and horse droppings around the post. But it was too cold today. Huddled in the sutler's doorway, arms about each other for warmth, we pressed our noses against the glass (what a miracle was glass!) and watched Mr. Casey wind a string of tinsel around a small pine tree.

"That tree is dead," I told Kingfisher. "Why does the sutler hang glass beads and popcorn and red balls on a dead tree?"

Kingfisher was a Sioux boy a couple of years younger than me, about twelve. Perplexed, he shook his head.

"My people do nothing like that, John Beaver!"

"Nor the Cheyenne," I agreed. "It is very strange."

Even in the doorway the wind pierced our

clothing like a driven nail. Reverend Parsley got only a hundred and thirty-eight dollars per pupil each year from the Government, and there was little money left, he said, for warm clothes. I had a ragged old cavalry greatcoat over my thin shirt and pants, and Kingfisher had to make do with a kind of cape from a condemned Army blanket. While we were huddled there, teeth chattering and noses running, a fat lady—one of the officers' wives, I think—pushed us aside.

"I declare—little vermin! Why, you're everywhere, aren't you, standing around and loafing while the Government supports you!" Still complaining, she swept by us into the store.

Looking at the tinsel-draped tree, I said, "I suppose it is an offering to their *Heammawihio*—the Wise One Above."

Kingfisher was mad at the fat woman. Gathering a handful of frozen horse droppings, he flung them into the air. "Old she-cat!"

Across the quadrangle the cavalry began to form columns for Saturday morning parade. From the dark sky whirled and danced the first flakes of snow. A band started the tune they called *The General* while yellow flags snapped in the wind. In their big fur coats the troopers looked like bears. We disliked them, Kingfisher and I and the Indian boys at the school. My grandfather had told me about them and what they had done to our people on the Washita and at Sand Creek.

But we were boys, and loved a parade. Though forbidden on pain of whipping to visit the parade ground, we ran joyfully for the music, dragging our trash sacks after us. Panting for breath, wiping our noses with our sleeves, we waited in a grove of skinny bare-branched cottonwoods at the edge of the parade grounds.

"Here they come!" Kingfisher giggled, wriggling like a puppy. I hunkered down beside him, blowing on my fingers. "*Esh piveh*," I giggled. "This is good. They will not notice us here."

On they came, a grand sight even if they were our enemies. First the mounted band, horses blowing snorts of steam. Horns blared, the big drum thumped with a beat that made our hearts march also. After the band came F Troop, and then B Troop, shiny horses prancing. Across the field the colonel commanding Fort McPherson sat his mount red-faced and stiff, looking the chief bear in bristling coat and cap with earflaps.

The sergeants turned in their saddles and bellowed at the men. "Right front into line— *ho*—o!"

It was all so beautiful; the columns breaking into fours, riders spurring up to join their mates in a long squadron front. Sabers snapped out and poked into the sky as the troopers passed the colonel. "Eyes right!" and each bearlike head swiveled round, as if pulled by a long string. It was *sha, sha*—beautiful. Only in dreams had I seen anything so beautiful. But as is well known, the best things in dreams can not be put into words.

Kingfisher was pounding one fist into the other in time to the passing drums, black eyes shining. "John Beaver," he said, "my uncle has a drum like that. Bigger, I think. I saw him make it from scraped horsehide, bound round a willow hoop. It is a loud drum; all the men dance to it when we go to war!"

The flank of the squadron was swinging past us now. The line of troopers seemed to stretch to the Iron Mountains beyond which my grandfather and my people lived.

"I must dance," Kingfisher muttered.

"What?" Surprised, I turned toward him.

"I must dance!"

I called a warning, but he did not hear. His eyes were bright, almost feverish. Scrambling to his feet, he ran from the tangled cottonwoods, body bent like a tight-strung bow, fists at his sides.

"Come back!" I called, "Come back!"

It was no use. Kingfisher whooped a war cry, feet patting the ground like a rabbit's as he shuffled about in a circle, head down, intent on his dance.

The troopers said an old cavalry horse could smell an Indian a mile away. I remember a red-faced Irishman from F Troop who told me all

Indians were dirty, and smelled like earth and smoke and grass. I can not speak for the Sioux but the Cheyenne are always clean, taking a bath in the river every morning to wash away bad spirits before the business of the day. Whether the near horse could smell Kingfisher, or whether his small dance scared the black, the result was the same. With a steamy whinny the horse reared, eyes rolling white. Coming down, he fell sidewise and one flying forefoot caught the next horse in the ribs. That one, a mean-looking gelding with a hammerlike head, kicked the next one in line, and that one his companion.

In an instant the whole squadron-front maneuver was broken to pieces. Men shouted and swore, sawing at the reins and trying to keep clear of each other. Along the once-perfect line horses kicked, bucked, bit, snorted, and butted. Some tripped and rolled to the ground, riders jumping clear and watching the scene with unbelieving eyes. In the dry winter air dust rose in clouds. The music of the mounted band went off-key, dwindled, and then stopped, except for a lone horn that kept foolishly on. The squadron was a shambles. Sergeants galloped this way and that, yelling and shaking their fists. It looked like a fight, what my grandfather, Strong Left Hand, called "gravy-stirring."

Kingfisher stood at the edge of the cottonwoods, staring at what he had done. I grabbed his arm and pulled him into the tangle of branches. The snow was coming down thicker now, and we blundered away unseen through the thicket.

"What—what happened?" Kingfisher asked. He was scared, I could see that. His lip quivered. Indians aren't supposed to cry, but they do sometimes—believe me.

"No time to talk about that now," I muttered, pulling him after me. Overhead a faint disc in the clouds marked the sun. It was time for us to be at our dinner in the Indian Salvation School.

"I didn't do anything!" Kingfisher howled. "Stop pulling my arm!"

We were both in trouble, big trouble. Although the dancing had been Kingfisher's idea, Reverend Parsley would punish us both. Dragging him after me, I skirted the stables and came round to the school from the other direction. The air smelled bitter. This day had started off *ohohyaa*—bad, very bad.

Reverend Evan Parsley ran the Indian Salvation School. I don't know why, but when an Indian is a bad man (and we have them, too) it shows in his face. He can not help it, and all people distrust and avoid him. But the superintendent was a kind-looking man with pink cheeks and a ruff of white hair round a bald dome. It came as a shock to me and Kingfisher when we saw him whip David Running Bear for stealing sugar.

Indians like sweets; my grandmother always made *mishkemaimapi*—sugar from boiling down box-elder sap—every spring. At the school we dreamed of sweets; *mishkemaimapi*, or perhaps the little cakes of sarvisberries, plums, choke-cherries, and currants, all pounded fine and pressed into flat squares to dry in the sun. But at the Indian Salvation School there was little food, and no sweets. No sweets, that is, except for the sugar Reverend Parsley kept in the pantry for his coffee. David Running Bear could not stand it, and one night broke into the pantry to gorge on forbidden sugar; that is why he was beaten, and afterward locked in the corncrib for a long time.

Scared, Kingfisher and I sat down to the wooden tables in the mess hall. If David Running Bear had been beaten for stealing a little sugar, what must be our punishment for having gone to the parade ground and caused so much trouble? I was shaking with fear, though I tried not to show it. I was glad my grandfather was not there to see me. He never showed fear of anything or anybody, except perhaps of certain spirits.

"What's wrong, John Beaver?" Kingfisher asked. "Where is the food?"

By this time there should have appeared the big black kettle holding what they called "stew"—a boiled cornmeal mush with scraps of salt beef, bones, and grease. The cooks always brought it in and sat it on a table at the front, and we filed by

11

with our bowls. But no kettle appeared, no cook, no platters of hard bread and pots of coffee.

"I don't know," I whispered back.

Bad news comes fast. Could the news of our sin already have traveled to the school? Silently we waited—thirty-five Indian orphan boys, all with heads down and hands folded in laps. Eyes darted this way and that, though, and a faint murmur arose, as old leaves rustle on a tree.

"I'm afraid," Kingfisher whimpered. Then he caught himself, adding, "Oh, just a little bit! Not much. I guess maybe I'm not afraid at all, now that I think of it. That feeling in my stomach is just hungry pains."

"There's nothing to be afraid of," I explained. "They won't know who did it, anyway. Indians all look alike; that's what the whites say."

The murmuring grew louder. One of the older Crow boys muttered, "We're hungry! Where's the food?" But that is the way with Crows. They are big talkers. They steal everybody's horses, too, and are always causing trouble. We heard there were even Crow scouts with Yellow Hair, whom we called *Pettin Hanska*, at the big battle on the Greasy Grass River only a couple of years ago. Well, what can you expect from Crows?

"It's coming!" Kingfisher blurted.

I looked up. Sure enough, there was the big black pot carried along by the Indian cooks. But after the cooks came Reverend Parsley, and with him was an 8th Cavalry officer, a skinny shaven-headed man with sweeping gray mustache and hard eyes.

When the cooks had placed the stew on the table, Reverend Parsley put his hands under his coattails, the way he did before making a speech.

"I know it's messtime," he said, "and I know you're all hungry. But first there's a little business we have to tend to. It won't take long—that is, it won't take long if you'll all help out and be good and responsible people the way the Government is trying to teach you to be."

He looked round in his pleasant way, but we were not deceived.

"There was a disturbance on the parade ground this morning," he went on. "No more than an hour ago. It seems that some Indian boys from the Salvation School disrupted the Saturday morning parade. The colonel is very angry and has sent his adjutant to investigate." He nodded toward the hard-faced officer. "Three animals were injured, and had to be destroyed. One of the troopers received a broken arm, and others suffered cuts and scrapes."

He paused, looking about. "You all know the parade ground is strictly off limits. Therefore, some boys in this room have committed a sin. In the interests of preserving their Christian souls, will these boys speak up?"

There was a silence, a deep and lonely

silence. No one spoke; the only sound was the wind whistling about the shabby buildings of the school. The hard-faced officer chewed his mustache, and helped Reverend Parsley look about.

"Come, now!" the superintendent urged. "This is a chance to show how civilized and agreeable you are all learning to be here at the Indian Salvation School. It is a good chance for the colonel to see how responsible we can be. The colonel is an important man in Washington, and can do much for the school."

Further silence; a bare-limbed tree in the compound scratched against the wall, and the sound made us jump. Beside me I could feel Kingfisher tremble. He pressed against me as if to gain courage, and cleared his throat.

"Shut up!" I said between clenched teeth. "Don't say anything, you fool!"

"But—"

"Shut up!"

The colonel pointed a long forefinger at me, and Reverend Parsley's head swiveled on his fat neck. "Did you speak, John Beaver?"

My Cheyenne name was Beaver Killer, for something that happened when I was very small. But they never let you keep your own name. Reverend Parsley had christened me John Beaver.

"No, sir," I muttered.

"Are you certain?"

14

"Yes, sir."

The adjutant made an impatient gesture, but Reverend Parsley put a hand on the blue sleeve with its yellow cavalry piping.

"Now I'm sure," the superintendent said, "that you boys realize the seriousness of this offense. It would be a shame if all were to suffer for the transgressions of a few. I shall give you one more chance. Who will tell me who the criminals are?"

The tree scratched again, and from faraway came the faint music of a bugle playing "Pease Upon a Trencher." The soldiers were eating. No one spoke. Kingfisher pressed tighter against me. "Should I—"

"Shut up," I said again. "Remember David Running Bear! Besides, they don't know who it is. It might have been anybody."

The silence in the room pressed so tight it hurt my ears. I said a little prayer to the Wise One Above. I hoped he was not busy at his own dinner, and so did not hear me. *It is not a sin,* I pointed out. *Heammawihio, it was an accident! Besides, some of their soldiers have been hurt, and horses too, though I regret the horses. On balance, is that not good, and in your honor?*

Reverend Parsley's face became red.

"All right, then!" He clenched his fist. "Brown sinners that you are, you shall feel the wrath of the Lord this day!" He made an angry motion at the gawking Indian cooks. "Take it away! Take away this nourishing food the Lord hath seen fit to bestow on us!"

When the poor cooks hesitated, he gave one of them a push that sent the man sprawling. "Take away the food! No food for sinners! Take it away, I say!"

The adjutant tugged at his mustaches, looking worried. "Now wait a minute, Parsley! I mean to say—is that altogether fair? After all—"

The superintendent mopped his face with a handkerchief.

"Captain Germany, I am humiliated! That the boys should have done this in the first place! And now, in the second place—" Gasping for breath, he stammered. "And in the second place, they refuse to give up the sinner! Why, why it's—it's Beelzebub's work, that's what it is!"

With sad eyes we followed the exit of the huge iron pot. It wasn't good food, but it was all there was. And young boys become hungry very quickly.

Parsley turned to us, shaking his finger.

"You shall not eat—sinners shall not eat! There will be no food until I am told which of you committed this act against our benefactors!"

One of the boys at a front table—probably a Crow—asked: "No—no dinner?"

The superintendent turned on him like a bear in early spring.

"No dinner! No supper! No *anything* till the culprits are identified. Is that clear?"

Still breathing hard, the superintendent took the officer's arm and pulled him away. We all sat there a long time, staring at the splintered wooden surfaces of the tables, white and dead-looking from their nightly scrubbing with lye water. Finally, one by one, we got up and wandered away to the dormitory. We had a half day off on Saturday. A half day to rest, to think, to decide what to do. Something had to be done; we were starving.

That was a long afternoon. We all lay in the dormitory on our cots and pondered. It grew colder, and the snow came down thick so that the room was filled with a weak gray light. Wind whistled, and snow leaked round the edges of the windows and fell on the floor inside. At one end of the room was a small stove, but there was little wood. If you got more than a step or two away, you couldn't feel the heat at all.

Henry Big Lodge said, "I don't know who did it, but he ought to confess. I think I'm dying from hunger. Already I feel dizzy."

The Crow boy who had spoken up in the mess hall shouted: "Someone here has a bad heart! Who is it?"

A boy called Bear Louse went downstairs and returned to report the door had been locked from the outside. We were prisoners.

Time passed. Frank Tall Bull said, "I wasn't there, I don't know anything about it. But it would have been fun to see the soldiers all mixed up and breaking their legs and everything."

Bear Louse was bitter. He was Arapaho, and they are always complaining. "That's fine for you," he said, "because you're fat and can live for a long time without eating, like a bear during the winter. But look at me!" He pulled open the coat to show his ribs. "I'm very thin, and need to eat pretty soon."

At five the bugles at the post blew "Pease Upon a Trencher" again, and we groaned. Even boiled mush and bones began to seem in remembrance like a delicacy.

My cot was near a window overlooking the post. I knelt beside it, blanket drawn over my shoulders against the cold. It was dark now, winter dark that came early. The snow was falling thick and hushed; the wind had died, and through the flakes I saw faint yellow lights winking from the cavalry mess hall, from the stables, from the commandant's big house. It is lonely to sit in the dark, cold and alone, and watch warm yellow lights through the snow.

Kingfisher hunkered down beside me, brushing snow from the sill with the back of his hand. Not looking at me, he said, "I think I ought to tell. My uncle was a war chief of the Oglalas, and he explained to me that a chief must do a lot of things for the good of his people. Of course, I am not a chief, but someday I might be. So it is good to do these things, even now."

Tattoo sounded. Nine o'clock already! Nobody had eaten since the scanty breakfast of bread and coffee at six. A few minutes later came the sound of Taps, faraway and muffled in the snow. It was supposed to be bedtime for us Indian boys, too. Everyone had talked and argued so much during the afternoon that they were tired, even more tired than hungry. Soon most crept into their beds and were asleep. Kingfisher lingered beside the window. After a long silence, he said, "Well?"

"Well, what?"

"I think I ought to go to Reverend Parsley and tell him I did it. It's not fair to keep everyone else from eating."

"All right, go!" I told him. "If you're going to be a war chief of the Oglalas, it will be good practice for you. But I'm in it too, remember, and you'll get me beaten along with you!"

He was younger than me, and always asked my advice. Now he hesitated; he started to say something, then changed his mind. For a long time he lay in his cot near the window, hands behind his head, watching the snow drift down. After a while I heard him breathing with his mouth open a little, and knew he was asleep.

Well, he was right; I knew that. Chief or not, making someone else suffer for your mistakes is not a good thing to do. But still I remembered the beating of David Running Bear. Also, I felt annoyed that a younger boy should tell me what was right, even if he spoke the truth. But how could I resolve this mess? What could I do?

Fasting was a good way to bring dreams. The Cheyenne depend a lot on dreams to tell them what to do. But I was already fasting, and no dream had come. A man in our tribe once stood neck-deep in the cold river for three days till he had a good dream, but the closest river was miles away. My grandfather's friend High-Backed Wolf used to make a sweat lodge and stay inside till he was wrinkled and pale-looking. He said that made good dreams. Others boiled certain grasses and berries, and drank the juice. But none of these methods helped me.

Finally I thought of something. My grandfather, when he had a hard decision to make, used to pull a coal out of the fire and sprinkle some sweet grass on it. Then he would crouch above the coal with his blanket over his head and breathe the smoke. That gave him a "good heart," he always said, so he would get the right answer and do the good thing.

I looked round. Everyone was asleep. There were snores and gurgles and deep breathing. At the far end of the room one of the young ones whimpered in his sleep; others groaned, probably with hunger, and tossed in their cots. But they were all asleep, even Kingfisher.

I had no sweet grass, but straw from the sack on my cot might do. A long time ago I had stolen a block of matches from the kitchen, and saved them against a time of need. Carefully I wadded up straw on the floor, cupped my hands over the match so the flare would not be seen, and lit the straw. Then I pulled the blanket over my head and crouched under it.

I must say it didn't smell very good. The smoke was hot and stung my eyes, and made me cough. But I stuck to it, crouching at the foot of my bed and breathing in the smoke. After a while I became dizzy and started to fall over. I had to brace my hand against the windowsill, but I kept on breathing smoke. Maybe I was about to have a good dream.

My senses reeled. In spite of myself I coughed more, and had to stuff a corner of the blanket in my mouth. Lights flashed in my brain, and I heard queer noises. Was it a dream, a good dream? Was *Sweet Medicine* himself coming to talk to me? Or was it perhaps a *mohin*, the hairy horned lizard man who seizes people when they have done something bad and drags them away to drown them in a lake? I shuddered, and breathed more smoke. I had gone too far to turn back now.

Suddenly a vision came to me. Maybe thinking about the *mohin* and his hairy face had done it. I saw again, as in a dream, the whiskery face of the colonel's adjutant, the one who had come to the school to complain.

Delighted, I threw off the blanket and sat up, gulping in cold sweet air. That was it! I would go to Captain Germany, the adjutant, and confess! Whatever the army did to me could not be as bad as being whipped like a cur dog! I would insist I was the dancer, the only one involved. After all, Kingfisher was only a child. If Oglala chiefs did a lot of things for their people, regardless of what happened to them, a Cheyenne could do no less. Someday I might be a chief, too. The Cheyennes have great chiefs. What was so great about Kingfisher's uncle?

Though we were locked in, I knew how to escape. Carefully I raised the sill and looked down. No one around; good! It was cold out there, colder than in the dormitory, but I climbed out, let myself hang from the sill by my hands, then dropped the dozen feet or so.

The snow had piled up beneath the window, and I fell into it without a sound. Quickly I was up, running around the dormitory to the trees at the back. They had been planted to shelter the building from the hot sun of summer; now I was grateful to hide among the bare trunks. Gasping for breath, I peeked round the largest tree. Snow and silence, and a faraway wink of light from the windows of the colonel's house. Next to it, I knew, was the smaller house of Captain Germany, the adjutant.

No Cheyenne ever stalked the night as carefully as I approached the adjutant's house. Running from tree to tree, I closed the distance. Once, at the corner of the stables, two troopers blundered by me carrying a bottle from the sutler's store. They were singing, and too drunk to notice me. Another time I fell flat in the snow and stayed quiet while a party of officers and their ladies came out of the colonel's house and said goodbye after a party. They stood on the porch a long time, talking and laughing. I huddled in the snow, whispering bad things about them, wishing they would leave. After a while, still talking and laughing, they passed by me. The talking and the laughing dwindled to silence, and they were gone toward Officer's Row.

Quickly I got up, shook off the snow, and ran up on the porch of Captain Germany's house. He was a bachelor, living alone with a Negro housekeeper named Emma White. We all used to think it was funny, a black woman named White. But we liked Emma. She used to give us a stick of candy to carry parcels for her from the sutler's store. When she came to the door I burst in, covered with snow, shouting, "I want to talk to the adjutant!"

Wide-eyed and open-mouthed, Emma stared at me as if I were a *siyuk*, the ghost of a dead person.

Then she said, "Oh, it's you! John Beaver. My, you look might near froze! What you doin' out on a bad night like this, boy?"

"I want to see the adjutant!" I insisted.

"What for?"

"It's—it's a private matter," I said, rubbing my hands together to warm them. In a corner the iron belly of a great stove glowed red, and I went toward it and turned to heat my backside. "It's important," I said. "Please hurry."

In one way I was proud of what I was going to do, and in another I was scared about the things I had set in motion. What was I—Beaver Killer, now named John Beaver—what was I doing in the lodge of a high officer of the white soldiers? For a moment I knew panic, and was ready to bolt into the night. But a door opened, and Captain Germany came into the room.

"What's all this, now?" he grumbled. He was in a long white nightshirt and cavalry boots, carrying a newspaper and looking at me over the tops of his spectacles. "Emma, what's this boy doing here?"

She giggled. "I doan know, sah. Bettah you ask him!"

"Please, sir," I said. My voice came out high and thin. "I did it!"

He pulled the spectacles down with one hand and glowered at me. "Eh? What's that? Did what, god damn it? What in hell you talking about, boy?"

My whole body felt cold and hollow, as if I were a pot filled with snow water. Trembling, I repeated, "I did it! I scared the horses, sir! I alone—just me—John Beaver, from the Indian Salvation School!"

For a minute he didn't say anything, just stared at me. By working his jaws he got one corner of the big gray mustache into his teeth and chewed at it. Finally he pointed at me with the folded newspaper.

"You, eh? Little rascal! Caused the U. S. Government a hell of a lot of trouble, that's what you did!" He slapped the newspaper into his palm. "Why did you do it, eh? Tell me that! You kids aren't allowed on the parade grounds! You knew that, didn't you, John Beaver? Well, why in the hell—"

"Cap'n," Emma said.

He swiveled, looking at her with one woolly eyebrow higher than the other.

"He cold," the black woman said. "Look how he shivering! Please, sir, lemme get a blanket to put round him, and a hot cup of tea!"

Captain Germany snorted. "Emma, this is a serious matter! I—"

But she was gone. He shrugged, wiggling his eyebrows. "God damn woman! What were we talking about?" He scratched his chin. "Oh, yes!"

Again he pointed the paper at me. "Now about this morning, boy. It seems to me that—"

Just then Emma came back and wrapped me in a red Hudson's Bay blanket. I sipped the tea and was grateful. Captain Germany, still sputtering, followed me to the stove where Emma put me in a chair and wrapped the blanket about my feet.

"All right, then," the adjutant grumbled. "Why in hell did you have to come *here?* It's up to Parsley to handle school discipline—he knows that! God damn it, you put me in a peculiar position, John Beaver! What do I—"

He broke off. Somewhere a bell was ringing, a fast and worried clanging.

"I mean," the adjutant said, "why in hell—"

Cocking a hairy eyebrow, he broke off, head to one side, listening.

"The fire bell, cap'n!" Emma cried.

The adjutant dropped his newspaper and rushed out on the front porch, nightgown flapping round his skinny legs. Emma ran after him and I came last of all, dragging the blanket.

"Listen!" the adjutant ordered, holding up a hand. "Three, four—*five!* Why, that's the school, Emma! The Indian School!"

Beyond the stables I saw a red light in the sky. It was the school, all right. I stood there gaping. A terrible feeling came into my chest.

"Cap'n!" Emma called. "Come back!"

He was already gone, striding away into the snow in his nightshirt, big boots making holes in the snow. Lights winked on in the stables, and in the glow of coal-oil lanterns the soldiers wheeled out the red fire pump and pulled it away toward the school, yelling and laughing. There hadn't been a good fire for a long time.

"My stars!" Emma wailed. "He ain't got on his pants, even! Why, he catch his death of cold!"

She hurried inside to get some clothes while I stood on the porch, turned to stone. Fire at the school! I knew what had happened, I didn't need any spirits to tell me that. In my search for a vision I had dropped my blanket on the still smoldering straw, and it caught fire. Somehow, while all the boys slept, the flames had caught at the straw pallet, and then crept up the wooden walls. I closed my eyes, trying to blot out the vision. *Ohohyaa*—bad, very bad!

"My goodness!" Emma wheezed. She rushed past me, fell off the porch in a snowbank, then got up and staggered through the snow, holding some clothes in her arms. "Oh, my stars and goodness! Why, it be the death of the man!"

I couldn't stay here, that was a fact. Wrapping the red blanket about me, I made for the hill behind the colonel's house, a rise that over-looked the post, the school, the whole settlement. Kingfisher and I used to sneak up there some-times and make medicine.

27

Now I saw the scene more clearly. One end of the dormitory—the end I slept in—was in flames. Below, the soldiers worked the levers of the hand pump, squirting a tiny jet of water. At the far end others propped a ladder, and my schoolmates were climbing down. I thanked *Heammawihio* for that, anyway; I had not burned up my friends.

Captain Germany's white nightshirt was near the hand pump, and beside him I could see Reverend Parsley waving his hands and yelling in the light of the flames. He was very angry. Breaking up the squadron parade was one thing; setting fire to the dormitory was another! My heart was sick.

After a while the flames flickered and died. There was only a little steam and smoke coming from the ruined end of the dormitory. A lot of lanterns bobbed about, and in their dim light Reverend Parsley was getting the Indian boys together; probably going to call the roll.

I knew what that meant; it was all finished. I could never go back there. But my grandfather's village was fifty miles west, beyond the Iron Mountains. Bleak and covered with snow, they were very high. Some thin clothes, a pair of cracked shoes, a red blanket still around my shoulders from Emma's generosity—no food, a few matches in my pocket. That was all. On the other hand, there was no choice. When morning came, they could track me easily through the snow. I would have to flee now, covering my tracks as best I could.

Before I turned up the rocky slope toward the west I took one last look. Now almost everything was dark. The fire was out and the excitement was over. In the front window of Reverend Parsley's house a candle still burned. I remembered that candle. It was in the middle of a wreath of greenery, and on a silken ribbon it said *PEACE ON EARTH*. That was a joke! There would be no peace till the white men left us Cheyennes alone!

CHAPTER TWO

My father and mother, my grandfather told me, were killed on the Washita, more than a dozen years ago. Since then my grandfather, Strong Left Hand, and my grandmother had raised me. They called him Strong Left Hand because his right hand had been almost chopped off at that same battle on the Washita. He had to learn to do everything with his left hand. He was a stern and dignified man, keeper of the Sacred Arrows, and I was always afraid of him. But my grandmother was different. She was a fat woman, very jolly; she was my *Nish-Ki*, and I loved her.

My grandfather remembered everything about the Washita, although I had been too small to remember. The horse soldiers, he said, rode into the Cheyenne camp shooting and killing, in spite of having given their word to let the people (the *Tsistsista*, as we called ourselves) stay on the Washita a little while. The white Colonel Hazlitt at Fort Cobb, my grandfather said, told the Cheyennes that if they stayed in their camp on the Washita, they would not be bothered. "Then," my grandfather would say, raising a forefinger and looking hard at me, "the horse soldier Hazlitt sent troopers into our camp from all directions! They had music with them—imagine such a thing—

and *Pettin Hanska* commanded the attack. The music was playing, and they killed hundreds of the *Tsistsista.* But only eleven of the killed were warriors, my son! Think of that! It was women the soldiers killed, and small children!"

I would hunker down in the gloom of the big lodge, arms wrapped about my shins, eyes fastened on my grandfather.

"That day," he would say, "began the decline of the *Tsistsista*! Dishonor was brought on the Sacred Arrows. Our ponies were stolen, our lodges burned, our food scattered for birds to eat."

I knew the story by heart, and loved it in the way children love to be frightened. True, my father and mother died on the Washita, but I did not remember them. Grandfather and *Nish-Ki* were the only parents I knew.

"Yes," I murmured. "And then came the coughing sickness."

My grandfather nodded. "That is true. *Ohohyaa*—very bad! And a lot more people died that winter."

Always the story ended the same way.

"Son, never forget this story! Never forget that the white colonel sat at Fort Cobb and planned this thing, all the time telling us everything would be all right, and that we did not need to worry." He took me by the shoulder each time and clasped it fiercely, looking into my face with

31

his old shiny eyes, surrounded with wrinkles like a dried-up creek bed in summer. "At the Greasy Grass we killed *Pettin Hanska*—the one called Yellow Hair—but the devil called Hazlitt is yet to be punished!

"This bad thing the colonel did to the *Tsistsista* started our long road down! Before that we were a great people. Now—" He covered his face with a fold of the blanket; the voice seemed to come from far away. "Now—now we are weak and helpless! We live as poor people, and fear everyone. Now the white men are trying to make us come into their reservations and live like farmers."

After that, my grandfather would say nothing for a long time, while the fire burned low. Silently I would steal away, closing the tent flap after me. I did not forget; I would not forget; I could not forget. Not ever.

Still frightened, I would run to the flat rock beside the stream where *Nish-Ki* would be scraping a wolfskin or pounding berries into a paste to be sun-dried for winter. My grandmother always called me *Mok-so-is*, which means "pot belly" and is a favorite word for little boys. "*Mok-so-is*," she would say, "what has that old man been telling you? Bad stories again?" *Nish-Ki* would comfort me, and tell me about *Sweet Medicine*, the Cheyenne god who first brought the Sacred Arrows to our tribe, or about

32

Thunder, the god who appears as a great white bird, or about her own childhood when there were no white men, no war, no bad times.

From *Nish-Ki* I learned something interesting; I had white blood in me. Oh, not very much; according to *Nish-Ki* (who was my father's mother) a French trapper named St. Onge came to the Cheyenne camp a long time ago and married my other grandmother. If that was true, it made me one-quarter white, but that was enough to put queer blond streaks in my hair. My skin was light, too, almost light enough in winter to pass for white, and my eyes were a pale color that in a certain light looked blue. Some of the boys used to tease me about it but although slight for my age I was the best wrestler in camp. Soon they gave up their taunts and became my friends.

Those were happy days. I rode a stick horse about the camp, swam like a fish in the meandering river, hunted rabbits and birds with my small bow and arrows. Sometimes we would beat the river for fish while our elders caught them in baskets. Other times I would stay by myself and make small boats of birch bark to sail on the river; I loved boats.

In winter we made sleds of buffalo ribs and coasted down the slopes. Then, too, was a great time for playing the "wheel game." We would all line a snowy hill, shaking our small lances.

A boy at the top would roll down a wheel made of a sapling bound into a circle and covered with a wolfskin, the whole decorated with ribbons and shells. The game was to throw the lance at the rolling, bounding wheel, and to "kill" it by pinning it to the ground with the lance. I got very good at this, too.

Summers were best, though, especially the Moon When the Horses Get Fat. In the morning I would wake to the shouts of the camp crier, telling the news of the day. "There will be a Willow Dance tonight" or "No one should kill buffalo today" or "The daughter of Picking Bones Woman is now letting forth blood, and is a woman."

I did not understand this last, or why such females had to stay away from the camp in a special lodge. But it did not bother me greatly. I would eat dried meat and berries from the buffalo-horn dish *Nish-Ki* gave me, and then rush out to see what was going on.

Already most of the young women would be gathering wood, digging roots, or plucking berries. The men sat before their lodges; smoking, nipping hair from their faces with mussel-shell tweezers, or telling stories. My good friend was Standing Alone, a girl my age who was the daughter of Doll Man, the camp crier. Even if she was a girl, she was tall and athletic, and good at breaking horses. She was the best in camp, and would drive them into deep water where they could not buck and jump. Then she would climb carefully on them, and talk into their ears. She would not tell anyone what she said, and everyone thought it was magic. But magic or not, she broke the wildest of horses. Already she had three of her own which had been given her as fees.

The autumn I got my name of Beaver Killer, I was with Standing Alone. It was very cold, and a scum of ice lay on the backwaters of the river. Close to shore I saw a fat beaver swimming with a sapling in his mouth. Gently, very gently, he cut a trail through the ice as he swam. Beaver is good meat, and I waded in with a rock in my hand, intending to kill him. But he saw me and swam away. Not wanting to lose him, I threw myself in the icy water and paddled to cut him off from the lodge of sticks and mud near the dam he had built. Standing Alone would never let me outdo her, and she dived in too.

Together we swam toward the startled beaver, and he dropped the sapling and dived. Laughing and excited, we dived too. In the murky water I could see the fat body and wide tail heading toward the underwater entrance to the lodge.

It was very foolish; to this day I do not know why I did it except to show Standing Alone how brave I was. A beaver has sharp teeth and claws, and when cornered he is dangerous. But I swam recklessly toward the dark hole and followed my quarry into it.

It was black and airless in there, and I regretted what I had done. The hole was small, and the sharp sticks lining it prevented me from backing out as I wanted to do. Frightened, I threshed about in the blackness, and by chance caught the beaver by the hind leg. I could feel him twisting, trying to escape, but I hung on.

"Help!" I shouted. "Help! I've caught a big beaver!"

Of course, no one could hear me.

"Grandfather!" I shouted. "*Nish-Ki*! Help!"

The place smelled awful. It was wet and dark and muddy, and stank of dead fish. But still I hung on. There was nothing else to do.

"Help!" I roared. "Someone come help me!"

In spite of my hold on his foot, the beaver managed to turn and bite my wrist. In pain I straightened, though still holding on. Cramped from bending over so long, I stood up and my head broke through the top of the beaver house.

Foolishly I stood there, gaping. A few feet away Standing Alone was thigh-deep in the icy water, staring at me. People came running from their lodges, and someone killed the beaver with an ax.

"You were very brave," Standing Alone told me.

I didn't feel brave, I felt foolish, standing there muddy and exhausted. What a crazy thing to do! But my grandfather was proud. He gave Doll Man a side of venison to walk around camp and tell everyone how Strong Left Hand's grandson had killed the beaver. That was how I got my name—Beaver Killer.

When I was twelve I left these happy times and went away to the school at Fort McPherson. I did not understand what it was all about. *Nish-Ki* did not, either; I remember she and Grandfather had a big fight about it. But the old man insisted I go. He had heard that white men were starting a school to train Indian boys to learn trades and become farmers and mechanics. Someone in Washington thought that was the way to make peace with the tribes; to take away the children and bring them up in the white man's way, to keep them so busy learning carpentry and growing cabbages they would not have time to cause trouble. I was angry and upset, but so in fear of my grandfather that all I could do was look sullen.

"What?" the old man barked. Sitting cross-legged in our winter lodge, banked about with snow against the cold, he leaned forward and gave me a hard look. "You don't want to go? But I tell you you *must* go! Your father was a chief, boy, and it is up to the chiefs and the sons of chiefs to do good for the people."

Though my chin trembled, I forced myself to look him in the eye.

"How do I do good for the *Tsistsista* by going to a white man's school and learning how to plow fields and make tin pots?"

The old man was firm. He had dreamed a dream, he said, and that was the way things were supposed to be. "Someday, when you are bigger, I will explain to you," he said.

In the face of my grandfather's dream, there was nothing I could do. *Nish-Ki* was sad to see me go, but she too respected my grandfather's dreams. He was known among the Cheyennes as a strong dreamer, a man who always dreamed good and true things. So I went to Fort McPherson and the Indian Salvation School, Grandfather himself taking me.

I never knew the feeling of loneliness till my grandfather got ready to leave. "Remember," he said, putting a hand on my shoulder, "you are Cheyenne, boy! That is what you are, and will always be. You are *Tsistsista*! Walk straight, always tell the truth, and learn all you can." Then, very stiffly, he got on his horse. An Irish trooper from Fort McPherson tried to help him, but Grandfather stared at the man with such anger that the cavalryman fell back and crossed himself against the power of my grandfather's scowl. Then the old man was gone, a blanket-wrapped figure disappearing in the trees along the river.

Never before had I been away from Grandfather and *Nish-Ki*, and it was a shock to me. But at that age, boys are tough and springy, like a hickory whip. Gradually I became accustomed to life at the Indian Salvation School. I parsed sentences, learned to cipher, chopped weeds on the school farm, and developed a skill with the adz and hand plane and saw. Along with the rest of the boys, I also learned a lasting hatred for the Reverend Evan Parsley, superintendent of the school. With the others I wondered how this hard and cruel man could have such a good-hearted daughter. She was pretty, I suppose, according to the white man's standards. Cora was older than I and inclined to her father's roundness of body, with corn-silk hair and gentle blue eyes so pale they were almost colorless. But she was a sweet and soft-hearted female who helped us with our lessons, and grieved when we were punished. It was Cora Parsley who first read to me the sonnets of Shakespeare.

Now that was all behind me. For better or for worse, I was free. It had been foolish for my grandfather to expect me to learn anything at that school, dream or no dream! He would be disappointed when I returned, of course, but I had had a dream too. I dreamed of seeing Standing Alone again; of playing the wheel game with the other boys, of snaring trout in the streams, of eating deer meat and tasting fresh-gathered chokecherries. I was going home!

Balanced against that wild feeling of freedom was the knowledge I was in a bad situation. Even if the soldiers from Fort McPherson did not chase me through the snow, it was still fifty miles across the mountains to my grandfather's village. I remembered a trapper caught in a blizzard the first winter I was at the Indian Salvation School. Henry Big Lodge and I were splitting firewood when two F Troop soldiers brought in an odd-shaped bundle. Inside was the body of the unfortunate trapper, frozen hard into the position he had died in, rolled in a ball, knees drawn up to the chin and arms wrapped around booted legs for warmth. That was the way the trapper had died, frozen like a piece of meat left outside in the Big Hard-Face Moon. Henry Big Lodge and I left our wood-splitting to follow the troopers as they carried the body to the adjutant's office.

"It's ridiculous," one trooper insisted, "and goes against nature to manipulate a corpse! We ought to dig a little round hole and just drop him in the way he is."

The other trooper shook his head. "Thaw him, I say, and put him in a pine box! Why, I'd never forgive meself if the poor man was condemned to roll through the Pearly Gates all tuckered into a ball!"

Captain Germany settled the question. They poured hot water over the corpse till its limbs softened. Then, after straightening the trapper out, they wrapped him in a blanket and put him outside to freeze straight, the ground being too hard right then to dig a proper grave.

Remembering the trapper, I shuddered. I didn't want to be frozen into a ball. Somehow I would survive, though I didn't know exactly how.

Fortunately, the snow stopped falling during the night. A pale moon came out, ringed with a ghostlike glow, and the wind died. I was alone, the only sound the shuffling my feet made as I walked through the blanket of white covering the world. Above me on a rocky peak a coyote howled. Another took up the howling, and then another. I said a little prayer. *Brothers, this is your land, I know that. I am Tsistsista, a friend of the coyote. I am only passing through here, and intend no harm.*

Intend no harm! Well, if the coyotes didn't know that, I did! I could not harm a rabbit enough to make a dinner of him. Not a weapon of any kind did I have. My boots were in fair condition, I still had on my ragged blue cavalry coat with the brass buttons, and over my shoulders I had draped the red Hudson's Bay blanket that had belonged to the adjutant. But that was all I had.

Telling myself that what I need do was simply keep putting one boot in front of the other, I stumbled on. Though the wind had died, the

41

cold pierced like a thorn. Wrapping my arms about me, pulling the hem of the blanket over my face so the air was warmed somewhat before I breathed it, I shuffled on. The yelps of the coyotes died in the silence behind me, and I said, *Thanks, brothers.*

Sometime during the night my feet became like blocks of wood. My legs still forced them up and down, into the snow and out, but there was no feeling in them. *Ohohyaa*—very bad! Nevertheless, I had to go on. The sun would soon rise, and the soldiers be after me. On I stumbled, head down, red blanket trailing after me. Where I breathed on the blanket wrapped round my nose was now a heavy crusting of ice, and I pulled the blanket off my head. But the air I breathed made my chest hurt, and I realized I might be freezing inside too. I wrapped the blanket around my face again.

On a rocky slope high among jumbled rocks I stopped, unable to go farther. Out of breath, I paused to look about me. The moon shone on a wasteland, broken only here and there by giant boulders rearing like fierce animals ready to devour me.

Sweet Medicine, I prayed. *Come help me. Show me the way.*

I sank into the snow, pulling the blanket around me. Trying to save warmth, I curled into a ball. *Just like the trapper, Sweet Medicine* said to me.

Just like that foolish trapper. Get up, boy! Move about. Light a fire!

A fire! Of course! Numb fingers searched my pockets, and found the block of matches. There was a way to start a fire in winter, in the snow. My brain moved slowly. What I really wanted to do was lie down in the snow and sleep. Freezing was not such a bad way to die, perhaps. But then I would never see *Nish-Ki* again, and Standing Alone, and Grandfather! Desperately my fingers brushed away snow as I fumbled for wisps of dry grass.

Thank you, Sweet Medicine, I muttered. *Thank you for your advice.*

Under the snow I found shreds of dry juniper bark, and some twigs. Shaking the snow from them, every movement of my body slow and awkward, I formed them into a pile. My fingers would not shape themselves to tear a match from the block, so I put it in my mouth and ripped one free with my teeth. Finally I got it in my fingers and scratched it, dropped it, and watched a little puff of smoke as the match fell and went out.

A little more help, I suggested to *Sweet Medicine. I need just a little more, and then I will take care of myself.*

Another match, another scratch, another failure. The match sputtered, sizzled, and went out. Angrily I threw it away, and bit off a third match.

This time I succeeded. Holding the match in

trembling fingers, I poked it into the grass and twigs. It caught, went out, smoked, then caught again and burst into flame.

It is enough, I said to *Sweet Medicine. Thank you very much.*

That night I made endless searches under the snow to gather grass, twigs, bark, anything that would burn. The fire was small and smoky, but by huddling near it, I managed to last out the night. At dawn I was red-eyed and weeping from the smoke, but I lived. I had come through a great trial, and Grandfather would be proud of me. We were *Tsistsista*, my grandfather and I and all the rest of us. We knew how to prevail.

The next morning all I could see of Fort McPherson was a smudge of smoke on the eastern horizon. Hungry and desperate, climbing among boulders at the top of the ridge, I was like a wild animal looking for prey. The blink of the sun on the fields of snow hurt my eyes; by noon they were swollen almost shut. Bruised, scratched, one heel torn from my boot in a fall, I clambered higher and higher, lungs laboring in the thin air. The sun became hot, and I tucked the folded blanket in my belt like a tail, carrying the cavalry coat over my arm. The sky was like a great blue bowl, so blue it made my head ache. Far away to the west, rising like a finger, was the slender spire of Rainy Butte. That was the direction of my grandfather's village.

Near the summit I paused, hearing voices. What could humans be doing up here, in this rocky waste? Cramming a handful of snow in my mouth to satisfy my thirst, I looked this way and that, trying to catch the sound, but it was not repeated. Perhaps I was dreaming. Maybe this was *Sweet Medicine* himself talking to me. I swallowed the snow water, and went on.

Slipping and falling, I toiled on, finally coming out on a flat shelf of rock. The sun had passed overhead, and was now sliding down the sky toward the west. Ahead of me lay the blue-gray bulk of the Iron Mountains, outline softened with a mantle of snow. When a shadow passed over my head I ducked, throwing up one arm. It was a great eagle.

This is your country, too, I said. *I am only passing through and mean you no harm.*

He dropped again through the sky to examine me, coming like a bullet. At the last moment his wings spread wide, braking his descent. With a ruffling sound the powerful wings pumped and he rose lazily upward, satisfied. A moment later and he was a dwindling speck, flying in the very top of the blue bowl.

An eagle is good luck, and very powerful medicine: *now,* I thought, *everything is going to be all right.*

Voices again! In the silence following the eagle's departure I could hear them. They sounded like children babbling, or women talking—a foolish yammering sound. Now there was no doubt. I could hear the voices plainly. Frightened, I turned to flee. Voices meant danger. But my feet remained rooted in the snow. Where there were human voices, there must be human food. I was frightened, but even more hungry. Whatever danger the voices meant—hostile Crows or Indian-hating white men—I made up my mind to risk it. After all, why survive a blizzard and then die of hunger?

Below the ridge was a sheltered tree-fringed area basking in the sun. Stumbling along the ridge I went closer, thinking the voices came from the small clearing. I was right; they were louder. Dodging from one rock to the other like a chipmunk, hiding and looking and then hiding again, I reached a ledge overhanging the clearing. Cautiously I poked my nose over. There, directly below me, was a rough pole corral, and in it were—goats!

Unaware of me, they dug with their hoofs in the snow, wrenching out tufts of grass and chewing, beards waggling to and fro, bleating to each other in goat language. Here were the human-sounding voices I had heard. Nearby was a rude shelter dug into the rocks, part weathered boards, the rest chunks of sod and branches. From a mud-and-twig chimney drifted blue-gray smoke. At some distance from the house, if you could call it a house, was a black hole in a cliff wall, spread about with piles of rock, weathered timbers, rusty picks and shovels, an old wheelbarrow. No Indian I knew would stoop to digging holes in the ground. This was a white man's place.

Other than the goats and the chimney smoke, there was no sign of life. In the snow I could see fresh tracks leading from the dugout into the trees. Whoever lived here must have risen early, perhaps to go along a trap line. There were no return tracks.

Cautiously I climbed down from the ledge. Goats have sharp eyes, and in an instant they discovered me and set up a gabbling. I paused, watching the dugout, but no one appeared. Then I climbed over the pole corral and among the goats, making soft noises to soothe them. From the school I knew goats and cattle and pigs. Though they were foolish and unpleasant animals, unfit for a Cheyenne to associate with, I nevertheless had a way with them. Gradually these goats lost their fear of me, and in the friendly way goats had, began to gather round, rubbing against me and watching me with their large pale eyes.

It annoyed me, thinking I had left farmering behind, but I picked one of the cleanest-looking females and wriggled beneath her, holding rear hoofs in one hand and stripping her udder with the other. I was starving, and the warm rich milk dribbling into my mouth meant life itself. The female bleated and kicked and shifted about as my none-too-gentle hands yanked at the teat, but I clung fiercely, squirting the stuff down my throat, as a baby clings to its mother's breast. Milk is not a proper drink for an Indian; at the school we never had milk, all of it from the herds being made into cheese and butter for sale to the soldiers at Fort McPherson. Nevertheless, nothing had ever tasted so delicious.

Almost I had had enough. The female was squalling and leaping about, trying to get free. The rest of the herd was nervous, too, and set up a whining to wake the dead.

"All right," I muttered, wiping my mouth with my sleeve. "All right, old lady. Thank you anyway, and goodbye." Giving her a slap on her rump, I sat up to find myself looking into the barrel of a musket propped on the top pole of the corral. At the far end of the musket was a pair of bloodshot black eyes, a red-veined nose, and a thicket of dirty whiskers.

Milk still dribbling from a corner of my mouth, I scrambled to my feet. But when the gun waved menacingly I stood still, afraid to move.

"Why, ye little varmint!" the whiskered man cried. His voice was hoarse and furry-sounding. "What in hell you doing here with my goats?" He watched my goat trot about the corral, shaking her head and complaining. "That's Sophie. If ye harmed her any, I'll—I'll—"

"I didn't hurt her," I explained. "I was just hungry, that's all. I haven't had anything to eat since yesterday morning."

He climbed over the poles, still holding the gun on me, and grabbed me by the collar of the cavalry greatcoat.

"What in hell are ye anyway?" He squinted hard at me. "Talk proper English, don't ye? Injun?"

Nothing I could tell him would help my case. Instead, I hung my head and stared down at my broken boots. But he gathered a handful of my long hair and pulled my head back.

"Where did ye come from, eh? Answer me that!"

Suddenly, forced to stare upward at the whiskered face, I knew him. He was a miner called Jake Noggle, who sometimes visited Fort McPherson to buy whiskey from the sutler. He was a troublemaker, and Captain Germany often put him in the guardhouse to sober up. There was a story he had attacked one of the laundresses, but I didn't understand that. The laundresses were fat soapy women with stringy hair, and I did not see how they could attract even the most desperate man.

"From—from nowhere!" I gasped, trying to pull back from the hairy face. His breath was like an old bear's when it gets up from its winter sleep—foul and rotten. "I—I was just—traveling!"

With an oath Noggle threw me away. The goats scattered in alarm. "All right," he muttered. "Whatever ye say would be a lie anyway, I reckon, and ain't worth listening to." With the gun he motioned to the dugout. "Get in there, and no tricks!"

I didn't want to go into that place.

"Please—" I begged.

He caught me on the cheek with the muzzle of the gun, and the front sight raked a cut across the face. I felt blood dribbling down my cheek.

"Will ye git?" Noggle roared.

There was nothing else to do. Inside the dark foul-smelling dugout he lit a candle and pushed me into a rickety chair. Then he bound my wrists before me, tying my ankles to the legs of the chair. Holding the candle high he knelt beside me and stroked my bare arm, chuckling. "Ain't a bad-looking young 'un, wherever ye come from!"

I shrank back in terror. Though I was young, I knew something of men like Noggle.

"Don't be skeered," he laughed. "I ain't about to harm such a likely boy!"

"Get away from me!" I snarled, pushing at his chest with my bound hands.

He only laughed, touching my cheek with rough broken hands. "Little catamount!" he chuckled. "I'll tame ye, or my name ain't Jake Noggle!"

I don't want to talk about the rest of it. All I want to say is that Jake Noggle sat in the dugout the rest of the day, drinking rum from a wooden keg, sloshing it a pint at a time into a rusty tincup. Sunlight wheeled in through the open door, marching across the dirt floor like the hour hand of a clock. Jake giggled and drank, smoked a few pipefuls. Every once in a while he staggered over to my chair and tried to fondle me.

I worked at my bonds till my wrists were raw and bleeding, but the miner did not appear to notice, being drunk. Around sunset I got my hands free, and managed to walk my chair about enough to reach the table on which was a tin plate with some dried-up stew, a coffeepot, and a butcher knife. Moving quietly so as not to wake him, I got my ankles free and stood up. Bound so long in the chair, my limbs were sore and aching. For a moment I almost fell, but I got hold of the butcher knife.

Noggle snorted, waking from his drunken dream. He rubbed his eyes, peering. "God damn it—wiggled out, eh?" Arms outspread like a grizzly, he lumbered toward me. I tried to evade him but he was between me and the door. His breath stunk in my face, and his whiskery lips were wet and red. Flinging his arms about me, he pressed me down on the dirty straw pallet in the corner. "Don't fight me!" he muttered. "God damn it, boy, quiet down a little, will ye? I just want to—to—"

The butcher knife had gone in hard, low down

between the ribs on the right side. Scared, he raised his body from me, propped on his arms. Blood began to drip from his mouth, stringy bubbles of red blood. "Eh? Stuck me? Is that what ye did, boy?"

I rolled out from under him, still holding the knife. Groaning, Noggle rolled over, the bed creaking under his weight. I had dealt him a death wound, I knew, but would he not die?

Sitting on the edge of the pallet, holding his side, he stared at me. He spat fresh blood, and wiped a hand across his mouth. "Why did ye do that, boy? I had no thought to harm ye! All I wanted was to—to—"

With a great effort he swayed to his feet, outspread fingers smeared red where they were pressed against the wound. His face changed; his eyes narrowed and the lips poked out from the thicket of beard. "Damned little rattler! Stung me, did ye?" He fumbled behind him for the musket, which he had propped against the chair.

Desperate, I remembered an ax that hung above the twig-and-mud fireplace. I tore it from the leather thongs, and while he was fumbling with the musket, I hit him in the head with the ax. He gave a horrible cry and fell, face upturned and arms spread wide. In the thicket of beard the mouth worked, making mewling noises like a cat. I hit him again and again, until the mewling stopped, and then hit him some more. Finally, my arms grew tired and almost in a daze threw the bloody ax away from me, as far as it would go, into a canyon where it clattered down and down and finally disappeared.

The spire of Rainy Butte was sharp and clear in the rays of the setting sun. The goats, anxious for feed, trotted around me, bleating and pressing against my legs. After what I had done, I felt sick. But there was no time to think about it. I took the musket and ball and powder, some dried meat and the butcher knife, which I stuck in my belt. I ate the dried-up stew on the tin plate, too, and drank cold coffee from the pot. Then once more I headed west, toward Rainy Butte. No white man could ever force his will on me again. I was going home.

CHAPTER THREE

Now I was better prepared for the journey to my grandfather's camp, but a joking *mohin* was putting obstacles in the path, laughing at my troubles. For one thing, it began to snow again. Not a blizzard, this time, but soft wet flakes that melted almost as they struck the earth, but finally piled into clinging banks that made the going hard. The skies were gray, and the wind became a soggy whisper. Once over the ridge where Jake Noggle's cabin perched, I now trudged across a rubbly plain where nothing seemed to live, not even a bird.

Something hurt in my chest, and I had to pause often to cough. I ate some dried meat and drank snow water, but on the third day my throat hurt too much to swallow. That night I found a hollow in the roots of a twisted juniper. Wrapped in my red blanket I burrowed down. Some animal had used it before me; the den was littered with droppings and smelled bad, but I did not care. I only hoped that, whatever the animal was, it did not return during the night to fight with me. I was too tired, too weak, to dispute the den with a chipmunk.

Near dawn I had a bad dream. I thought I still had that bloody ax in my hands. Harder and harder I swung, chopping Jake Noggle into flying bits of flesh and bone. But under the blows the miner's body changed. It was now *Sweet Medicine* who lay there, helpless. He covered his face, and died. I had killed *Sweet Medicine* himself. In fear I scrambled from the root-tangled den and ran into the snow. For a moment I stood cold and trembling, trying to remember where I was and what I was doing. Then reason returned. I shivered, wrapping my arms about me. In the half light of dawn I saw a figure like a huge dog moving among the rocks. As I watched the wolf moved away like a ghost, grayness lost in the grayness of rocks and the grayness of dawn.

Somehow I kept moving. I lost track of days and staggered on, coughing and nearly spent. At times I knew where I was and why I was there; at other times I became foolish with fever, shouting crazy words and laughing at nothing. Once I remember being very hot and flushed, even in the snow, and threw away my red Hudson's Bay blanket. That night I was sorry. A chill came on me, rattling my bones and making my teeth clash together. When morning came I did not think I could get up. But a remembrance of blue-coated soldiers came on me, and I ran shrieking down the hill, seeing the tall finger of Rainy Butte sharp and clear before me. I do not remember, but I *think* I called out to Grandfather and *Nish-Ki* to help me. It was cowardly, I know, but all I can say is that I was very sick.

For a long time after that I did not remember much. The first clear thing my mind could grasp was the knowledge I was in a warm place. Someone was feeding me broth from a horn spoon. It tasted good, and I grabbed at the spoon and tried to get more. But I was very weak, and a hand pushed me down on the skins again. I slept.

Then there was the doctor who came to the lodge. His face swam in my vision, but I screwed up my eyes and stared at him a long time. Finally I knew him; it was Lightning Man, a great healer from my grandfather's village. Was I home?

Had I finally reached my grandfather's camp? Excited, I tried to talk but he paid no attention, only going about his healing ceremonies. Finally I sank down again, too weak to do anything but watch.

Lightning Man walked about the lodge, shaking his rattle and singing a song to drive away bad spirits. Then he took a coal from the fire with his bare fingers and sprinkled juniper needles on it, rubbing his palms in the smoke. With hands warm and sweet-smelling, he knelt beside me and rubbed my chest and throat to draw out sickness.

"Am I in my grandfather's lodge?" I asked. "Have I come home?"

Lightning Man frowned at my interruption, but did not answer. From his pouch he took a twisted medicine-root and bit off a small amount. After chewing it well, he spat the ground-up root onto my chest, rubbing it in with his fingers.

"Where is *Nish-Ki*?" I demanded.

He paid me no attention. Singing his prayer-song, he sifted yellow dust into an old coffeepot, mixing it with a stick. Then he took from the pot a sticky stuff that smelled like deer fat, colored a bright yellow with the dust, and with his stick spread it on my forehead, my cheeks, my ears, the hollow at the base of my throat. As he daubed, he pointed with the stick to the four directions, calling them off one at a time. *"No tum—ho shin—hun so wun—so wun."*

I got sleepy after a while, but felt better. Lightning Man, I remember, sang several songs after that, but I did not hear all of them. I fell asleep.

From that time on, things became clearer in my mind. My chest and throat no longer hurt, though when I tried to speak my voice was like a frog's croak. *Nish-Ki* came to the lodge where I lay and held me in her arms as if I were a child. Comforting as it felt, I tried to struggle free. But I was too weak.

"Little *mok-so-is*," she crooned. "You have come back. What a hard trip it was! But you were very brave."

She brought me a cup of fish oil—a rich fat made by pounding fish bones to powder and boiling them till a clear white oil came to the top of the pot to be skimmed off. It did not taste good, but she made me drink it, saying, "It is good for you; rich and full of life."

I tried to tell her about Reverend Parsley and how I had fled from the burning of the school, but she pressed her fingers against my lips. "Not now, *mok-so-is*! There is plenty of time for that later. Now sleep!"

Mok-so-is, I thought, disgusted. *Pot belly!* She shouldn't call me that; it was embarrassing. But now that I knew *Nish-Ki* was near, I knew all would be well.

Time passed. It was warm and smoky-smelling

in the lodge. A fire always burned. About the edges of the lodge snow was heaped to keep out the wind. A shallow trench covered with twigs and branches and snow let fresh air come from outside and pass through the fire to the smoke hole overhead. Someone tended the fire, but whoever it was moved quickly and softly, and I did not know his identity. Then, one morning, I saw the person in the shaft of sunlight as the door flap opened. It was Standing Alone.

"So," I said. "It is you."

Dropping the wood she was carrying, she knelt beside me, touching my cheek with the lightest stroke of her fingers.

"You know me," she said shyly. She made the sign for happy—first the gesture for *heart,* then carrying the left hand out to say *day,* then both hands sweeping out and up in the sign for *sun.* Sunshine in the heart.

"Yes," I said. "I know you."

I was glad to see Standing Alone, but ill at ease. I, Beaver Killer, once strong and quick, was now an invalid, while Standing Alone, tamer of wild horses, hovered above me. Muttering, I turned my face to the lodge skins.

"Are you feeling bad?" she asked. "Shall I call Lightning Man? He will fix something to help you."

Angry and frustrated, I pushed her away. "No, I am not sick!" I howled. "Will you go away?

58

Someplace there must be a deer hide for you to scrape or a robe to quill!"

Astonished, she sat back on her moccasined heels.

"But I—I—"

"Go away!" I insisted, turning my face to the wall again. "I do not want to see you now." Later, I turned to look toward the door flap. The fire blazed with new wood, but Standing Alone had gone.

It took a long time to get up the strength, but one day I managed to rise shakily to my knees. My head swam and I was out of breath and sweating with effort. Finally I managed to stand up, holding the buffalo robe about my naked form. I had always been slender, and small for my age, but I was shocked as I looked down at my body. Skin and bones, I was, and not much of that. My knees were knobby and swollen, my ribs stuck out, my arms seemed like willow twigs. *Ohohyaa*—very bad! Maybe I had been sicker than I thought. With a stick of firewood for support, I tottered to the door flap and looked out.

All the world was white. The pines were heavy with snow; the branches drooped almost to the ground. The sun shone on the snow and it hurt my eyes.

Young as I was, I remembered the time when my grandfather's camp was a big one. Then the lodges were pitched in a circle whose diameter was three arrow flights from a strong bow, a half mile or more. What my grandfather said was true; bad days had come on the *Tsistsista*. After the big battle on the Greasy Grass River a lot of our people had fled with Sitting Bull to Canada. Many had died of the coughing sickness, as I nearly had. Others, feeling *Sweet Medicine* had abandoned us, drifted away to live with more lucky tribes. Now there were not many people left. But it was still good to look on the camp and watch the familiar daily activities.

From the lodges gray columns of smoke rose into the winter air. Women hurried to the stream to break the ice and carry home water in hide buckets. Older boys were driving in the herd of horses. The younger boys were skittering down the hills on their buffalo-rib sleds, as I had once done. And Doll Man, the crier, was shouting the news. On his spotted horse he began, as always, at the opening of the circle of tents, which faced the rising sun, and rode around, first to the south, then the west, then the north, and back to the east again, in each direction repeating the news. Even from a distance I could hear his droning leather-lunged shout. *The Contraries will have a dance tonight. This day no one is to hunt, because it is a sacred time for the animals and they must not be disturbed when they are talking to their own gods. High-Backed Wolf has lost a brown horse with four white feet and slit nostrils.*

It was good to see and hear these things, after being so long away. Blinking in the warmth of the sun, I stood a long time, holding to a lodge pole for support. I was still standing there when my grandfather rode up on his horse and got stiffly down, tying the animal to the thong of the tent flap.

"Well," he said, "I see that my grandson is on his feet again. *Esh piveh*—that is good." Though he had never been affectionate, he put his hand on my head, smiling.

"I am better," I admitted. "Now I do not need any woman to bring food and take care of me."

We went into the lodge and he waved me to my blankets. "Lie down and we will talk," he said.

I did not lie down. Instead I squatted in the bed, wrapping a skin robe about me. He did not comment, only sitting on his heels opposite me, wrapped in his blanket. Finally he took from his beaded pouch a short pipe, which he stuffed with sweet-smelling bark and lit with a coal from the fire.

"You were lucky," he said, "that my friend Gentle Horse was out hunting for a stray from the herd. He found you lying in the snow, and brought you back to our camp." He rubbed his nose with the carved stem of the pipe. "Almost you died. It was the coughing sickness. We were all afraid of it, and kept you in a separate lodge.

61

But your grandmother and the girl Standing Alone took care of you. They were very brave. Maybe you owe your life to them."

How frail he looked! He was very old—I knew that—but even with his crippled hand he had been strong and active. Now the hand shook when he held the pipe, and his voice was thin and rustling. Only in his eyes was there life.

"I guess it is time to talk," he went on. "Now that you are better, I would like to know how it is that you left the school and made this crazy journey over the Iron Mountains in winter." A ghost of a smile touched his lips. "Maybe you should join the Contraries."

It was the nearest to a joke he had ever come. The Contraries were a warrior society who always did things backward. If they meant "yes" they said "no." If you asked one of them to come near, he drew back. If he told his woman, "Do not bring in any more wood, we have plenty," it meant that the fire had gone out and she should cut more. In spite of their odd behavior, however, they were men of importance, entrusted with important duties. Some of them were camp chiefs, as was my grandfather, and others led the *Tsistsista* in war.

"I admit," I said, "it was a foolhardy thing to do. *Heammawihio* must have seen me and helped me, or I would have died. But it was necessary for me to do it." I went on to tell him how

Kingfisher and I had caused such commotion at the regimental parade, how I had confessed my part in it to Captain Germany, how I had accidentally burned down the dormitory at the Indian Salvation School and fled.

"Now," I concluded, "I have come home. I am very happy to be here. I do not want ever to go back to that school. Reverend Parsley is an evil man. I do not think I learned very much anyway."

Puffing his pipe, he looked at me through half-closed eyes. Finally he said, "There is more."

I fidgeted under his gaze.

"More? Something more?"

He didn't speak; just looked at me. I remembered I could never deceive my grandfather. It was not that I *could* not—after all I was smart, as boys go—but it did not seem right to do so.

"All right, then," I said. I went on to tell him the story of how I had stumbled on Jake Noggle and his goats, how the miner had tried to mistreat me, how I had stuck him with the knife and when he wouldn't die, killed him with the ax. Even now, the telling of it, long after, made me feel queer and uncomfortable.

"Ah," my grandfather said. "Well! All that happened, eh?"

He was still looking at me, sucking at the pipe. I went on, words tumbling out of me mixed with the signs that were sometimes useful when you couldn't put things into the right words. Once,

63

at school, Joe Pretty Bull and I had put some *Hamlet* into our signs, and it worked pretty well. Now the signs helped me tell something that was hard to put into words.

"Noggle was a bad man," I insisted, "and it was right he die. But there is one thing I do not understand, Grandfather. When a man is bad, it is necessary to kill him quick and get it over with for the good of the people. But I—I—" I stammered, groping. "After he was dead, I kept chopping him with the ax. I hit him again and again. Grandfather, I was like a *mohin*, crazy and evil myself!" I shook my head. "It was very bad, and I do not know why I acted so crazy. Do you understand?"

He nodded, knocking the dottle from his pipe.

"Then tell me!" I cried. "Explain it to me, please!"

In that unfamiliar gesture he put his hand on my head. "I do not wonder you do not understand," he said quietly. "Although grown up a lot since I saw you last, you are still young." He tapped his forehead with a finger. "Young in the head, that is to say. But old men like me have considered these things for a long time, and know why men act the way they do."

Fumbling in his beaded pouch, he brought out a piece of paper. It was a newspaper clipping—yellow and faded, so brittle he had to be careful not to break it.

"This school," he said. "They taught you to read the white man's language?"

"Yes," I admitted. "I am a good reader."

"Then read this to me."

It was a short piece from a newspaper called the Sacramento *Union*, dated several years back. At the top of the clipping was a picture of a stern-faced man in a military uniform, with sweeping mustaches and a hawk-like nose. The black headline said GENERAL HAZLITT TO SALT LAKE CITY. Below, in smaller type, was the story:

> General Wesley E. Hazlitt, U.S.A., War Department expert on pacification of the savage Western Indians, was assigned this date to command Fort Douglas near Salt Lake City, headquarters of the 6th Cavalry. The general and his daughter will take over the commandant's quarters in a month or two. Already the charming Miss Julie Hazlitt is planning a series of receptions for—

"That is enough," Grandfather ordered, holding up his hand. "Do you remember this man?"

"Of course," I said. "This is the man you always told me about—the man who planned the fight against us on the Washita—the man who had the women and children of the *Tsistsista* killed—the man who started the bad luck for our people!"

"Do you hate him?"

"Of course I hate him!" I burst out. "I hate all people who harm the *Tsistsista*! I hate all white men!"

His eyes glowed with an old heat. "Of course you do! So do we all, and we will make them pay for what they have done to us!" He got up and limped back and forth in the lodge. I had never seen him so excited. "They will pay!" he repeated. "They will pay!"

Almost youthful again, he squatted beside me. "This man Noggle—I have heard of him. He is a bad man. And he was trying to do to you a bad thing, like the white men are trying to do to the *Tsistsista*. He was trying to make you like a woman—weak and without will—as the white men are trying to do to us. When you were killing the man Noggle, grandson, you were killing *all* white men! You were killing Noggle, and your teacher at the school, you were killing every white man that ever harmed the *Tsistsista*!" He waved the faded clipping. "You were killing this evil soldier, too! That is why you were so crazy and wild! You were striking for the *Tsistsista*, for us all, for the Sioux and the Arapaho! You were killing the miners who dig holes in our mountains, you were killing the trappers who take our brothers the animals, the buffalo hunters who spread dead white bones all over our land! You were killing the lying white men far away in the place they call Washington, where they make bad pieces of paper and try to get us to put our thumbprints on them!" His voice became hoarse; he coughed, putting a hand to his throat. "That," he concluded, "is what you were doing for us, grandson. I am glad you told me." He coughed again, and spat, looking tired.

"Well," I said, "I am a *Tsistsista*. I will count coup on any man who harms my people. The Sacred Arrows demand it."

Grandfather's hand shook as he lit a fresh load in his pipe.

"You are a good boy. I thank *Sweet Medicine* for such a grandson. You must always remember the Sacred Arrows, and ask *Sweet Medicine* for help when you need it."

The Great One Above gave the Sacred Arrows to *Sweet Medicine*, and *Sweet Medicine* brought them down to the Cheyenne as a perpetual sign of the Great One's favor. For years my grandfather had been Keeper of the Sacred Arrows. They were kept in a Medicine Lodge built especially for them. Once a year there was a great ceremony when the Arrows were taken out and shown to the people. There would be singing and dancing, and the people would all make vows for the coming year.

"Now, then," Grandfather went on, "when you are well again, and go back to the Indian School—"

"Go back?" I was startled. "Go back to that—that school? Why, Grandfather, they would do awful things to me—beat me, even kill me! I burned down the sleeping place, though it was an accident! I can never go back there!"

Puffing deep on his pipe, cheeks sunk far in, Grandfather looked at me a long time. Finally he said, "They will not kill you. Beat you, maybe, but that is something you have to suffer for the *Tsistsista*."

My voice rose in a way it had never before done when talking with my grandfather. "How can it help the *Tsistsista* for me to be whipped like a dog by the Reverend Evan Parsley?"

"Soon you will understand," Grandfather said quietly.

"But how—why—"

He held up his hand. "I have had a dream," he murmured.

My grandfather's dreams were famous for their truth and beauty. In spite of myself I kept silent. His eyes were tightly closed, his face turned upward in the shaft of sunlight that came in through the smoke hole.

"I have had a dream—a great dream," he repeated.

I felt my skin prickle and crawl. The sun cast a holy light on my grandfather's face. It was as if he was talking with *Heammawihio* himself, high up on the Sacred Mountain.

"This great dream came to me a long time ago," he chanted. "It came to me out of a great storm cloud, where there was thunder and lightning. You know that dream, *Heammawihio*! You know it was a true dream, because it came down from your own lodge in the sky."

Being in the midst of sacred things taking place, I was frightened. I trembled, but Grandfather, eyes still closed and face turned toward the beam of sunlight, put his hand on my shoulder.

"Now look on this boy, *Heammawihio*—blood of my blood, bone of my bone, dream of my dream! Look on him, Great One. Is he not truly *ho nuh ka wa*?"

I knew what that meant. It meant someone dedicated, usually a man called to be Bearer of the Thunder Bow, the symbol of great power exercised for the benefit of the people. But I was only a boy—a boy who liked to play the wheel game, to slide down snowy hills in winter, to pretend at war with my friends in the willows along the river. *Ho nuh ka wa* meant to me the famous men of our tribe, people like Bull Head and Blue Thunder and Broken Dish.

"Speak, please," Grandfather said to the heavens. "It is part of my true dream, *Heammawihio*. Is this boy not *ho nuh ka wa*?"

The beam of sunlight suddenly quivered. I blinked my eyes, but it was no trick of vision. The golden shaft danced—it brightened, diminished, wavered, trembled—almost as if it lived. I blinked again, rubbing my eyes. Had a cloud passed over the sun? What had happened?

"Thank you!" Grandfather shouted. He grabbed my shoulder so hard it hurt. "Did you see that, grandson? He spoke! The Great One spoke!" He threw his arms about me, and pulled me out of the lodge to call to the people.

"Listen, everybody! It is coming true! This boy is *ho nuh ka wa*! The Great One himself has said so!"

All the people came running, crowding about Grandfather and me, patting my arm and stroking my cheeks. My grandfather was proud and excited, pulling me this way and that for people to look at and admire. But I felt very funny. In the midst of all the hubbub I looked up at the sky. It was blue, with not a single cloud in sight. Then I knew indeed that *Heammawihio* himself had been in my grandfather's lodge. *Heammawihio* himself had placed the Thunder Bow in my hand.

CHAPTER FOUR

From that day on there was steady improvement in my health. *Nish-Ki* cooked rich foods for me; I delighted in buffalo calf boiled with *pomme blanche* roots, or deer blood cooked in the rennet so that it set like white man's jelly. Now that it

70

was spring I gorged on the tender shoots of wild licorice and drank a lot of the tea she made from the leaves of the red-leaf wood. It was sweet; at that time it seemed I could never get enough sweet stuff. *Nish-Ki* said some people called the tea "red medicine," and it made a very good tonic for me.

I regained weight I had lost, and put on some more. My spare frame filled out, I grew taller, my voice deepened. The day came when finally I could join the other boys, playing at the coyote game, running through the line, and arrow mark. These were exciting sports I remembered with delight, but somehow they were not now the same; they bored me. Soon I began to wander away and stand, wrapped in my blanket against the April winds, to watch the girls play *oassiof.* They had a big ball stuffed with antelope hair. A team of players kicked it into the air and kept it there as long as possible by bouncing it on their insteps. Standing Alone was the best girl at *oassiof.* I could watch her all day; laughing, long hair flying, graceful as a deer as she danced about. When she had the ball, it seemed to have a life of its own, floating high like a bird with no help at all. And when, in the heat of the game, I saw her skirt ride high on her firm thighs, I felt a vague and puzzling discomfort.

"What are you doing?" *Nish-Ki* asked me one day.

"Nothing," I muttered.

But I was doing something. In a dark corner of the lodge I was whittling out a little flute from a piece of juniper wood.

Nish-Ki gave me a sly look. "Don't you think I know what a flute looks like? The first time I saw your grandfather I was in my father's lodge and I heard flute music. It made my heart beat fast, and I sneaked out to find who was playing." She looked into the fire but her eyes went far beyond, to a place and a time very distant. "That is what flute music does to a young girl," she sighed.

"I don't know about such things," I protested. "I just want to make a little music, that's all. I am tired of playing child's games, and maybe I will become a musician for our people. I will make a drum, too, and a rattle, and sing wolf songs to lift the hearts of the people in these bad times."

She only giggled, giving me a playful shove. Annoyed, I left the lodge, and finished the flute on a ledge of rock high above the camp, where no one could make fun of me.

Well, I was no longer a child. Things had changed. But there were other changes, too, that made me sit long hours on that rocky ledge, looking down at the camp of my people, thinking long thoughts. Though barely a youth, I was now an important person. I was a special person, a *ho nuh ka wa*. When I passed, warriors, elders of the tribe, important men—all averted their eyes in respect, and made sacred signs. Women drew their children from me, so as not to weaken my strength by blundering into the mystic aura that surrounded me. Even *Nish-Ki* became respectful; when I tried to joke with her, she only smiled in a quiet way and went about her lodge duties. I tell you, it was very unsettling, especially since I didn't know why this great honor had fallen on me. And I knew enough about my grandfather not to ask too many questions; my questions sometimes made him angry, even when they were about commonplace things. So this matter of being *ho nuh ka wa* was something I thought I had better not ask him about. In his own good time he would tell me. Probably it was just a preliminary to my succeeding him some day as Keeper of the Arrows. After all, he was getting old.

Anxious for someone to talk to, I played my flute one rainy night outside the lodge of Doll Man, the camp crier and father of Standing Alone. But she did not come. Disappointed, I stood for a long time in the rain, becoming so wet that *Nish-Ki* forgot my status and scolded me. It made me feel good, that scolding, but Grandfather looked sternly at her. She stopped talking and went back to scraping a deer hide with a worn chip of buffalo bone.

"It is *Mahkeomeshi*," Grandfather announced.

"The April Fat Moon. Are you well now, grandson?"

"I am well," I said.

"And ready to carry out your task—ready to go back to the white man's school, and wherever the Thunder Bow calls you after that?"

"I am ready," I said. Actually, of course, I was not ready. But when a person is *ho nuh ka wa*, he must keep silent and do only what is best for the people. I still did not see how going back to the school helped the *Tsistsista*, but my grandfather said it would, and he had had the dream, not I.

For a while he smoked his pipe in silence. *Nish-Ki* acted as if she wanted to say something, but he frowned at her. She only muttered and went back to the deer hide.

"I will have it announced all over camp," Grandfather said. "That will make the people happy. And soon we will have a Medicine Lodge to tell *Heammawihio* and *Sweet Medicine*. They will be happy, too."

A Medicine Lodge was a big event, held only when there was an important matter to be dealt with.

"*Esh piveh*," I murmured. "Very good."

But it was not good. Responsibility weighed on me like a stone. I was no longer a boy, a *mok-so-is*. Suddenly and unexpectedly I had been thrust into manhood. I couldn't think clearly, my brain was in such confusion.

Next morning the rain stopped. Everything was spangled with beads of moisture, and very clean and beautiful. I went up on the big ledge of rock and sat in the sun.

After a while I got a headache from thinking so much, and I took out the flute and played a song. I thought I ought to play wolf songs—the songs sung by young warriors who are traveling out as "wolves" or scouts to meet the enemy—but after a while I found myself playing *ta mis si va in*. It says, "Put your arms around me, I am not looking." What it means is the thoughts of a young girl. If she sees her lover about to embrace her, propriety demands she repulse him; but if she is not looking and he surprises her, then it is all right for the young man to take hold of her. It is a very gentle and sweet song.

Hearing a rustle in the sumac bushes behind me, I jumped. I was very nervous. But I did not need to fear anything. It was Standing Alone.

"I heard your music," she whispered.

Not looking at me, she sat down, plucking a few strands of grass and plaiting them into a pattern. "I heard you the other night, too," she added, "when it rained. But my father would not let me come. He said you were now *ho nuh ka wa*, and could not be bothered with girls." She looked up from the finger work, eyes concerned. "Is this true?"

What to say? I stammered for a while, not

acting dignified as I should, but finally managed to blurt out something.

"Well," I admitted, "I am *ho nuh ka wa*—that is true, I guess. And maybe I can not be bothered with girls. That is to say, just *any* girls, girls in general." Summoning up my courage, I touched her hand. The soft feel of it made me tremble. Before, we had played and wrestled and been close together, lying side by side in the grass as we stalked imaginary deer. But that had been different. "What I mean," I stammered, "is that— well, I am glad to be with *you*." Blundering, I rambled on. "That is to say, I have never thought of you as a girl, exactly. What I mean is—"

Angry, she knocked my hand away and stood up.

"I know what you mean! Well, this is a fine thing to say to a girl who risks her father's anger and sneaks away from his lodge just to listen to music from a flute!"

"No!" I cried. "No, that is not what I meant!" I scrambled to my feet, catching her wrist. "Listen to me! I am very lonely!" My chest heaved with a strange emotion. "I am lonely for *you!*"

I do not know how these things work. Somehow my hand drew her and I felt her soft body against me. Her lips sought mine, and our bodies were warm against each other. No, they were not warm; they were hot, like fire!

"And I," she whispered, "I am lonely for you,

too. I do not care if you are *ho nuh ka wa*! You are Beaver Killer, and I love you."

Below us there was a commotion in the camp. Doll Man ran from his lodge and peered about. Even from that distance I could hear his bellowing. Standing Alone trembled.

"Listen," I said. "What is the matter?"

"It is my father," she whispered. "He has found me gone."

With a quick press of her cheek against my breast she ran into the bushes, leaping over a fallen tree like a young doe. Then she was gone. There was nothing left but the warm feeling where she had pressed against me.

A few days later when Doll Man made his early morning round of the camp, shouting the news, I heard him cry that his daughter, Standing Alone, was now a woman. She had passed blood, and some day she would bear many sons to carry on his name and make him comfortable in his old age.

I never attended a Medicine Lodge before. In the first place, children were not allowed. In the second place, Medicine Lodges were not often held, being saved for great occasions. But now I, Beaver Killer, was to be dedicated to carry the Thunder Bow.

Half-frightened, half-eager, I sat on a dais of willow boughs in the center of the lodge. The

Dog Soldiers—one of our warrior societies, with numbers now pitifully small—were conducting the ceremony. They painted me with white clay, drawing a line of white down my arms and legs, a circle over my chest, and stars and a moon on my face. I wore a special deerskin tunic, tied about the waist with a red and white cord ending in a tassel. A bundle of fragrant sage was tied to each wrist and ankle, and in my right hand I held, like a scepter, a painted pole topped with a tuft of eagle feathers.

In the ceremony there were a lot of things I did not understand. For example, a buffalo skull was the central object in the lodge. A man called Young Bird, a good friend of my grandfather, put bundles of grass in the empty eye sockets, and with two sacks of paint, one red and one black, painted the skull. He drew a line of black between the horns, down to the nostrils. Then he paralleled that with a line of red. Finally he painted the whole left side of the skull red, and under the left eyehole a black crescent moon and a red sun.

A man called Shave Head took out a clay pipe and filled it with *kinnikinnick*, lighting it with a coal. He passed it all the way round the circle of Dog Soldiers. Each took a puff to purify himself, drawing deep before it was handed to the next man. When it reached me, I took a puff but it made me cough. Shave Head frowned and shook his head, taking the pipe from me and putting it back in its ceremonial pouch.

They all sat silent for a long time. Finally Spotted Hawk and Standing Elk and Yellow Bull got up and danced for *Heammawihio*'s pleasure, calling on him to take notice of the Medicine Lodge. Then Yellow Thunder and Pine sang wolf songs while other Dog Soldiers took a spade decorated with ribbons and went outside. By craning my neck I could see them cutting squares of sod, which they brought back into the Medicine Lodge.

As I say, I did not understand all these things, but one thing I did understand. That was the look of pride and joy on my grandfather's face. He sat in a place of honor, on a buffalo robe at one side of the lodge, and in the thick blue-gray smoke lit by patches of sun from the open smoke hole I could see his great happiness.

When the two men piled up the blocks of sod in a kind of altar, a buzz of excitement went through the people who had been invited to see the ceremony. Slowly, very slowly, my grandfather rose, the bundle of *Mahuts*, the Sacred Arrows, in his right hand. He was naked except for breech-clout and a blanket knotted around his waist. The breech-clout was a ceremonial one, long and dangling, back and front, richly ornamented with porcupine quills dyed in many colors. His chest and face were painted, too, with broad streaks of vermilion and ocher, befitting the Keeper of the Sacred Arrows.

Tall and dignified, he advanced to the altar, now covered with a red offering cloth.

"All people look," he said, showing them the bundle. "Be reverent. You are in the presence of the *Mahuts*." Painfully he sank to his knees before the altar, at the same time making a holy gesture toward the grass-stuffed eyes of the buffalo skull. "Turn away your faces, all people and I will let you know when to look. We do not want to offend *Sweet Medicine*."

The bundle was unwrapped and spread on the altar. At his command we all looked, averting our eyes at first so we did not seem too bold. I had never before been in the presence of the *Mahuts*, and I was frightened to be so close. There they lay on their bed of offering cloths and white sage; the six Sacred Arrows richly painted and feathered.

"On *Nowahwus*, the Sacred Mountain," my grandfather chanted, "the Great One Above, *Heammawihio*, first gave to *Sweet Medicine* the Sacred Arrows. They are a sign of the Great One's favor. But now we are out of favor with the Great One. There is blood on the Arrows. At the river called Washita our chief Black Kettle was tricked and murdered by horse soldiers. The high chief called Colonel Hazlitt tricked us, sent his men to slay women and children, drove us from our peaceful camp into the wilderness."

People murmured, speaking in asides to each other, moved by my grandfather's words.

"Ever since that day," Grandfather sang, "there has been blood on the arrows." He held the bundle high. "Look! Do you see? Blood on our Sacred Arrows!"

There was indeed blood on the Arrows. It was evident from where I sat—patches of dark red staining the shafts and feathers.

"Blood!" Grandfather chanted, waving the *Mahuts.* "Blood of our people, blood shed by trickery, sacred blood of the *Tsistsista!*" He trembled in passion. People began to cry and to mourn the dead, so unjustly slain. Some clasped their knees and rocked from side to side. One old woman, called Picking Bones Woman, took out a knife and cut her wrist.

"Since that time," my grandfather chanted, voice trembling with emotion, "the *Tsistsista* have come on evil times. We have been chased by our enemies, we have died from the coughing sickness, we have not been able to find the game we used to hunt, we have become a small and pitiful people. Now the white men are trying to make us to come in to their reservation and become farmers. Imagine that!" He shook his fist. "Farmers! The *Tsistsista!*"

My flesh crawled, my heart pounded. I knew now why my grandfather had been called a great speechmaker. The people were excited, calling out and pressing around him, trying to take his hand, begging him to help them in this day of sorrow. Some rolled on the ground in fits of rage and frustration; others prayed to *Heammawihio* and *Sweet Medicine* to help them. Watching, I could not help think of Cora Parsley and her Bible. She used to read to me and tell me about God and Jesus. *God and Jesus. Heammawihio and Sweet Medicine.* Did the white people get that idea from us?

"Tell us," the people implored. "Tell us what to do! How do we wash the blood from the *Mahuts*?"

Some were so excited the Dog Soldiers had to restore order. But finally the audience was calm, and my grandfather spoke in a quiet voice.

"You know me. You all know me. I always speak the truth. I am Strong Left Hand, keeper of the *Mahuts*." He held up his maimed right hand to show them. "I was there, at the Washita. That is where this happened to me. That is where the blood first came on the Arrows. And this is the truth; blood can only be washed away by blood. Many of us tried this, tried to count *coup* on the soldier Hazlitt, tried to wash the Arrows in Hazlitt's blood. But we failed."

Picking Bones Woman held up her hand. Red still dripped from it, falling on her skirt and legs.

"What do we do, then?" she begged. "Honored

old man, Keeper of the Arrows, what do we do?"

My grandfather closed his eyes. "I had a dream."

Everyone was very still. All the people knew that Strong Left Hand was a famous dreamer. For April, it was a very warm day; the interior of the Medicine Lodge was hot and stifling, filled with smoke and the fragrance of white sage and the smell of people. Beads of sweat formed on my forehead, dripped down my nose and the corners of my mouth, but I was not supposed to move. I sat stiffly on the dais, holding the painted pole with its tufts of eagle feathers.

"I had a dream. *Sweet Medicine* came to me in this dream and told me what to do. *Sweet Medicine* told me that the *Tsistsista* are getting weak and without will, and soon it will be too late. He told me a certain young man of the *Tsistsista* alone had the power to carry the Thunder Bow. He told me this young man was strong, that this young man would grow to be wise, like *Si No Pah*, our brother the fox, that this young man was born to be brave and do good things for the *Tsistsista*."

I began to be uncomfortable, and sweat some more. Was this I he was talking about? I did not feel very great.

"The chief soldier called Hazlitt has gone far away," my grandfather went on. "He moves among white men, near the great waters. For us, the *Tsistsista*, it is hard to come near him, because our color is different from him, and our ways are different from white ways, and we would be found out. But in my dream *Sweet Medicine* appeared to me, laying his hand on my grandson, Beaver Killer. *Sweet Medicine* told me to send away my grandson to Fort McPherson, where he would learn the ways of the white men. *Sweet Medicine* said that Beaver Killer, with his light eyes and streaky hair and French blood, could then follow the horse soldier Hazlitt wherever he went, going unnoticed, and one day would have a chance to wipe the blood from our Arrows. That was our chance, *Sweet Medicine* said, our only chance to become a great people again."

Everyone looked at me. I fidgeted, and swallowed hard. My nose itched from the sweat droplets, but I could not scratch. All I could do was sit there and look straight ahead, like a proper *ho nuh ka wa.*

Slowly Grandfather walked toward me, holding in his hand the sheaf of Sacred Arrows. Hypnotized by their power, I stared unblinking at them. Smears of blood danced in my vision; once more they became fresh and red, dripping their shame on my upturned face. Though I had been an infant at the time, I saw again the waters of the Washita, turned red by the blood of the *Tsistsista.* I heard the shrieks of the women and children, saw *Pettin Hanska* and his troopers in their fur coats galloping about the camp, burning our lodges, driving away our horses. I never remembered my mother and father, but now I saw them clearly. My father was naked, running out from his bed at the alarm, carrying a lance decorated with feathers. He fought bravely, but one trooper shot him from behind, and another knocked him down with the butt of a rifle. My mother ran from the lodge carrying my little sister, but she and Red Flower were ridden down and clubbed as they stumbled through the broken ice of the river.

"This is our hope," Grandfather said. He touched me on the head with the *Mahuts.* "This is Beaver Killer, the hope of the *Tsistsista.* He is our savior. Through him the *Tsistsista* will again become great."

Breathing hard, filled with emotion, I sprang to my feet and gave a great shout. Angrily I hurled the painted pole. It stuck in the middle of the ceremonial fire like a spear. Quickly the fire blazed up, almost as if in some kind of a sign.

"I am Beaver Killer!" I shouted. I slapped my chest, and stared fiercely about. "I am *ho nuh ka wa*!"

Confused and excited, caught in the grip of a passion I did not entirely understand, I ran from the Medicine Lodge into the trees. For three days and nights I stayed alone, without food or shelter, on a rocky outcropping above the camp. I had strange dreams, dreams that would take a long time to tell, let alone explain the meaning of. I was, I realized, a strong dreamer too—perhaps as strong as my grandfather. No one came after me; no one came to offer food, or water, or companionship. They understood.

When I came down from my fasting and dreaming, my grandfather had a horse ready for me, and some food and a small *parfleche* cylinder which he handled carefully. I knew what it was; I had often seen it tied to a cord around his neck. It was a rawhide container in which was a piece of the sweet root which represented to us the spirit of *Sweet Medicine.* Never before had it left the cord around his neck.

"Here," he said, handing it to me. "Take this. Pray to it when you are in trouble, and *Sweet Medicine* will come to you."

Even then, after the Medicine Lodge and all my dreaming, I was still a little confused and uncertain. It seemed I was a poor *ho nuh ka wa.* Great things were demanded of me, but I was not sure of their exact shape.

"Grandfather," I said, "when the time comes for me to act, how will I know just what I must do?"

"*Sweet Medicine* will tell you," he said. "Do not worry about it, grandson; when the time comes, you will know what to do to help the *Tsistsista.*"

He hesitated for a moment, one hand on my knee as I sat the beautiful painted horse he had given me. My grandfather, who was such a great orator, seemed at a loss for words. He started to speak, but his voice trembled, and he fell silent.

"I will not forget you," I said. "Nor will I forget the people, no matter where The Great One Above leads me."

He nodded. "I know you will not, grandson." Then he turned his head away, still with his hand on my knee. "And before you go," he said, "I hope that you understand why I have done these things. I hope you will at last know why I sent away my only grandson, why I wanted him to learn the white man's ways, to speak his language, to know his thoughts."

I could not speak, but there was no need to. He patted my knee again, and turned away.

Nish-Ki was there, too, and Doll Man and Picking Bones Woman and the Dog Soldiers and other people. I wished Standing Alone was there, too, but she was passing blood again and was confined for the monthly period to the "unclean" lodge, far away from the circle of lodges. In a sudden April change it began to snow. It was not cold, but little feathers of snow drifted down. Soon the waiting people were dusted with flakes of white.

"You will be careful?" *Nish-Ki* asked, trying to keep her lip from quivering. But emotion got the better of her. She rushed to me and clung to my foot where it rested in the stirrup of the old cavalry saddle.

"Yes," I promised, "I will be careful."

Grandfather pulled her away, lifting his hand in farewell. His hair and eyebrows were powdered with the snow, and all the people stood in the softly falling flakes and watched.

"Goodbye," I said.

At the turn in the trail I reined up and looked again. They were standing as before, motionless, watching me go, silent figures in the falling snow; the *Tsistsista*, my people. Fumbling in my pouch, I brought out the *parfleche* cylinder. *Help me!* I thought. *Sweet Medicine, help me to help my people.*

CHAPTER FIVE

In the April Fat Moon I rode back to Fort McPherson. The trip this time was an easy one, supplied as I was with a good pony and provisions. There was a little rain and some snow, but in the main the sun shone and the trees began to leaf out and the grass to green.

The post looked the same. For a long while I paused on the rise above the colonel's house, the same rise where I stood so long ago, shivering and scared, watching the sleeping place burn.

Now the weather was warm, but I was still frightened—more scared than I had been that snowy December night. I began to doubt myself and my resolve. To dig my heels into the pony's ribs and ride down there sealed my doom. I would be beaten, imprisoned, even sent to some white man's jail a long way off. Maybe—just maybe—I would be hanged! Once I had seen a hanging at the post. Kingfisher and I watched a trooper die—a bad man who had killed a bunkmate and then deserted. It was not a pretty sight. We had both been sick afterwards. But I was *ho nuh ka wa*; the Medicine Lodge had made me so.

As I neared the Indian Salvation School my limbs turned to ice. I could hear my heart thumping like a big drum, going faster and faster. I swallowed in panic, but forced myself to go right up to the door of Reverend Parsley's house and dismount. Maybe my heart would blow up and I would die right there. That was my hope, anyway. *Ohohyaa*—everything was very bad!

But it was not to be so. Some of the boys were raking up old leaves beneath the trees in the front yard. When they saw me they ran up, chattering and excited.

"John Beaver! Look, everyone—he has come back! Where have you been, John Beaver? Did you run away, after what happened? Why have you come back?"

Kingfisher was there, too, holding my pony as I got down.

"John Beaver," he whispered, "it was a mistake to come back! Oh, it was a big mistake!"

He was older than I remembered, taller and more grownup. They were all bigger. I got down from the pony and stood there, looking around. The burned-out end of the dormitory had been rebuilt, I saw.

"Why don't you say something?" Kingfisher demanded, grabbing my arm. "Are you sick?"

Well, I was sick all right. I did not trust myself to speak, even. Just then, attracted by the noise in the yard, Reverend Parsley came to the door.

"What's going on here?" he shouted. "Back to your work, all of you! Do you think the Government boards you to chatter and waste time? What—"

His jaw dropped open and he stared at me. Everyone fell quiet. A long way away, on the drill ground, soldiers were marching. In the silence I could hear the shouted commands of the sergeants.

"Well," the superintendent finally said, "John Beaver, eh? You have come back."

I found my voice, but could not look at him. "Yes," I said thickly. "I—I have come back, sir."

"Then," he said, "you know you are to be punished. And you know why you are to be punished. Is that not so?"

For a moment I thought wildly of trying to explain; of trying to tell him that I was sorry for having disrupted the parade, that the burning of the dormitory had been an accident; that I fled not because of guilt but because of fear. But a true dedicated man did not act that way. I raised my head, and looked him in the eye.

"Yes," I admitted. "I know why I am to be punished, sir."

"Then come with me," Reverend Parsley said. He waved angrily at the boys. "Get back to your work, all of you! This does not concern you!" He lead me away to the corncrib, where he locked me in with a big rusty padlock. "John Beaver," he said, putting the big ring of keys into his pocket, "this is where you will stay until I have decided what punishment is proper for the sins you have committed."

That was the way I came back to Fort McPherson in the April Fat Moon.

I stayed three days in the corncrib. The head cook, a Mexican named Zuniga, brought bread and water to me. I always liked him; sometimes in the lean-to kitchen he let me mix bread dough and chop up turnips and potatoes for the soup.

"I would bring you more," he whispered, "but the superintendent is always watching."

I looked toward the house, seeing a small movement behind the starched curtains.

"I know," I said. "And I thank you. *Muchas gracias.*"

Once or twice Reverend Parsley himself came, reading to me from the Bible. Then he said he was going to pray for my soul, and got down on his knees. But when I refused to do the same, he became angry.

"All right, then!" he shouted. "The Devil has you in his power, John Beaver! But there is a good way to drive the Devil from your soul, when you are so proud and stiff-necked!"

Now whatever made me refuse to get down on my knees? I had never been very sure exactly what a devil was, except that it must be something like a *mohin*. But I couldn't persuade my legs to bend to a white man's god, though it might have gone better for me. Miserable, I chewed on a crust of bread. The weather had turned cold again, and I had nothing on but the light deerskin vest and pants *Nish-Ki* had made for me.

That night I napped in starts, being too cold to really sleep. But about midnight according to the stars, I woke to find a warm blanket beside me. Wondering, I turned it this way and that. Who could have risked Reverend Parsley's anger to bring me a blanket? Zuniga, the cook? Kingfisher? Who? But the next day, when the superintendent came to pray for me again, he saw the blanket and took it away, being even angrier

92

than the day before, and surprised-looking, too.

"Who gave you this blanket, John Beaver?" he demanded.

Truthfully, I didn't know. But Reverend Parsley didn't believe me, and went away muttering to himself. I hoped no one would get in trouble because of me.

The morning dawned clear and blue, with a few wispy rose-colored clouds in the east. Somehow I had an uneasy feeling that this was the day of accounting, the day I would be tested. I still had the *parfleche* packet around my neck. Taking it off I held it up in the barred rays of sunlight coming through the slats of the corncrib.

Sweet Medicine, I prayed, *help me this day. Keep me strong and brave and worthy of the Tsistsista. Whatever happens, make me truly a dedicated man, like Bull Head and Blue Thunder and Broken Dish and all the great men of our tribe.*

I was not mistaken. That morning Reverend Parsley unlocked the corncrib and made me go into his house. I had never been in there before. It was a big cold kind of a place, only the bones of a real living place. He took me into his study, a dusty room with books on the shelves and a big globe of the world. On a windowsill was a bunch of violets in a water glass. *Cora,* I thought. *The superintendent would never pick flowers and put them in a glass. It must have been Cora.*

A picture of their Jesus hung on the wall. Reverend Parsley sat across the desk from me, looking at Jesus, not at me.

"Well," he finally said, "I do not want you to think, John Beaver, that I have decided on your punishment without giving it a lot of thought."

"Yes, sir," I said.

"I want you to know I have prayed a long time about this. I have gone through my own Gethsemane. The decision came not without great pain and struggle on my part, as it did to our Lord."

I didn't know what Gethsemane was, but it wasn't a good time to ask.

"You caused great trouble for the Army," he went on, "which is our benefactor here. Your carelessness and willfulness burned out one end of the dormitory. It is plain to see the Devil is in you, and must be driven out." He clasped and unclasped his hands, finally looking directly at me.

"Yes, sir," I agreed.

He blinked, eyes watery in the sun streaming through the window. Motes of dust danced in the light and I watched them.

"Is that all you have to say?" Reverend Parsley demanded. "Are you going to just sit there and say 'yes, sir, yes, sir'?" Maybe he was disappointed the Devil was not putting up more of a fight.

"Sir," I said politely, "I have done wrong, I guess. It is up to me to accept my punishment and get on with my studies. So I am ready for whatever comes."

After all I was *ho nuh ka wa*, a thing the superintendent could never understand. It was time for me to sacrifice myself for the good of the *Tsistsista*, as Blue Thunder and Broken Dish and the other dedicated men had done.

Somehow my acceptance made him mad. His face got red and he stood up, undoing the buckle of his belt. "Very well," he cried. "You must be whipped, then! We will drive out that Devil, John Beaver!"

He was a thick-set man, with a big belly. The leather belt was long and thick.

"Take down your pants, boy, and bend over," he ordered.

Although I had known it was coming, I was furious and ashamed. Look what *Sweet Medicine* had got me into! For an instant I thought of bolting for it, of running away. I was fleet of foot and might escape. But I knew I couldn't do that.

"All right, sir," I muttered. "I am ready."

I could see his shadow on the floor, arm raised to strike. Waiting for the blow, I set my teeth hard. When it came, it was delivered with a force that knocked me sprawling. The sound echoed like a cannon-shot through the house. The belt snaked round my buttocks, cutting as if a saber had slashed me. My senses reeled. I lay stunned, face pressed against the threadbare carpet.

"Get up!" Reverend Parsley shouted. "On your knees again, John Beaver! Beelzebub is not driven out so easily!"

Somehow I got to my knees again. When I fell I had cut my lip, and I could taste blood in my mouth. I put a hand to my face; it came away speckled with red.

"Yes, sir," I muttered, and bent over, "I—I am ready."

Blood, I thought. *Blood. They are shedding our blood again. Will they never stop?*

I saw the black shadow, arm raised high, outline of the dangling leather belt across the carpet, and I braced myself. Let it come!

"Aaagh!" A grunt was forced from him with the violence of the swing. Again the belt cut across my bare behind. This time I was ready for it and managed to stay upright, though pain rushed through my bones and skin even to my hair and teeth and fingernails.

Sweet Medicine, I thought in agony. *Where are you? Do you see me? How can you let this go on?*

"Now we are getting somewhere!" the super-intendent panted. "The Devil is getting ready to leave your body, John Beaver! A few more strokes and—"

That was when the door banged open. Someone

rushed to me, throwing her arms about me. I could feel curls against my cheek, smell the warm scent of a girl.

"Papa!" Cora sobbed. "No! You mustn't! Please, Papa, don't whip him! I can't stand it!"

A girl! Rescued by a girl! And me with my bare bottom showing! I was confused and embarrassed. Putting out my hand, I tried to push her away.

"Cora," I begged, "Cora! Go away, please. Not now!"

She clung to me, still sobbing, putting her body between me and the leather belt. "Papa, Jesus wouldn't want you to do this! Please, Papa!"

He tried to pull her away, but she clung like a leech. "No, Papa—no!"

"Cora, I order you to your room!" the superintendent shouted. He had a handful of her dress, and I heard a ripping sound as part of the bodice pulled away. Then I could feel a bare shoulder next to my cheek. Reverend Parsley's anger was fanned to white heat. He trembled with rage, and said a lot of bad things—bad, that is, for a Christian minister, though I had heard the troopers at the post use the words many times.

Well, he and I were united in our fury. Cora meant well, but she was interfering with my chance to do something for the *Tsistsista*, as my grandfather wanted me to.

"Go away!" I howled. "Oh, Cora, go away!

This is not your business! Go away, you silly girl!"

This time I did not see the shadow of the upraised belt. The only thing I knew was that the superintendent, in his rage and shame, had struck again. The whip curled about the both of us, and Cora, being a girl, cried out in pain and her body went limp. Having taken most of the force of the blow myself, I tottered and sprawled, falling across her. Briefly I shut my eyes against the blackness, waiting till the pain should stop washing through my body. When I opened my eyes, there was death in my hands. I would kill the superintendent! Shakily I got to my feet, pulling my pants up around my bleeding bottom, looking wildly round for a weapon. Something—anything! The heavy inkwell, the brass stand of the globe—anything! But I stopped, my twitching fingers stilled.

Never had I seen such a look on a man's face. Reverend Parsley was dumb with horror. His face worked violently, his body shook as with a palsy. The eyes were wide and staring, as if he had seen the Devil himself—and I think he finally had. He didn't seem to be aware I was in the room. "Lord!" he muttered. "Oh, Lord, Lord! What have I done!"

The belt dropped from his hand. He staggered forward, hands reaching out in a beseeching kind of way. "Cora! Child!"

I didn't know what to do. I stood there for a while, watching him huddled over his daughter's limp form. After the uproar and the shouting and the violence, it was quiet in the library. Motes of dust still danced in the sun. The curtains were white and starched. The globe still showed Africa on top, a dark patch against the blue of the oceans.

"Cora!" Reverend Parsley whimpered. He pressed her blond curls against his chest, rocking her like a child. "Cora, forgive me!"

She stirred a little, opening her eyes.

"Papa?" she whispered.

I felt sorry for the superintendent. I had been whipped on my behind but he had been whipped inside, in what he called his Christian soul, I think.

"Sir—" I murmured.

He didn't answer, only went on rocking her, tears splashing on her upturned face. So I went away, walking slowly back to the sleeping place. The boys had just come out of arithmetic class; they gathered around me, talking and laughing and wanting to know how I had gotten away. But seeing the look on my face they became silent, one by one, falling back before me as I walked into the dormitory and up the stairs.

My bed was still there, at the end of a long row of cots. I sat down on it, then got quickly up. My bottom was seething with red-hot little snakes of pain. After a while I took out the *parfleche* cylinder and held it in my hands. This was powerful medicine. This was *Sweet Medicine.* He had come to my rescue.

Some time later Kingfisher came silently up the stairs and stood beside me. I guess he noticed the blood on my trousers because he rummaged in a sack under his bed, coming out with a hollow section of buffalo horn with a vile-smelling paste in it.

"Let me help you, brother," he said.

Stretched out naked on my bed, I let him rub the salve into my wounds, trying not to cry out.

"It is something my uncle made for me when I went away to school," Kingfisher explained. Putting the wooden plug back into the horn, he sat for a long time on the edge of the bed, not saying anything. Finally he muttered, "We will kill Parsley some day, John Beaver—you and I!"

Head pillowed on my folded arms, I was grateful for the way the salve was beginning to draw the sting from my wounds.

"Yes," I agreed. "Someday we will kill all the white men, and get our land back."

It was odd, but after that I never had any trouble with the superintendent. He never even spoke to me, seeming to ignore me completely. But he was very fair with all the boys, and life at the Indian School became more bearable.

When I came back to school, I was nearly fifteen years old. Remembering my grandfather's desires, I stayed on there for almost two years, preparing myself for what would some day be an encounter with the horse soldier Hazlitt. At the school we got donations of used books, and they were often wrapped for shipping in old newspapers. From a six-month-old copy of the Los Angeles *Express* I learned that the general and his lovely seventeen-year-old daughter were still in Salt Lake City, cutting a wide social swath through the Mormons there, but that he was being considered for command of the Presidio in San Francisco. Somehow or other—I didn't know how—I must hurry. My quarry was fleeing farther and ever farther away.

I put my stay to good use, however. The first time I saw Cora Parsley after the incident in her father's library, I was still embarrassed and awkward. But she came forward with such a simple and natural goodwill, taking my hand in hers and walking with me toward the drafty shed where we had our classes, that I soon felt at ease. Neither of us mentioned the beating.

"I see," she said, "you are doing well in your studies, John Beaver."

"Well," I muttered, "I try hard, I guess."

"You have a good brain," she smiled. An early snow was falling, and the flakes nestled in her blond hair and on the shoulders of the wolfskin coat she wore. "It is more than that," she went on. "Papa says that of all the boys, you are the most likely to amount to something."

Against my will I had found myself thinking of the soft white shoulder under the gingham dress, the shoulder that had been against my cheek as she tried to protect me against her father's beating.

"Eh?" I asked, astonished.

"It's true," she laughed. "Oh, John Beaver, I wish you knew my father better! He is a good and godly man, though at times—" Her face clouded. "At times he is—is—"

"Violent," I muttered.

She took a deep breath; frosty little vapors came from her lips as she spoke. "Yes, I guess so. But it's because the Lord takes hold of him so strongly that he behaves so. He means well." She stood with me for a moment at the door of the classroom. Then she gave me a quick awkward pat on the hand and hurried back toward the superintendent's house, calling over her shoulder something about housework to do.

I was early to class, as I usually was. The professor, a man named Golightly, one of three elderly Christian pensioners kept on to teach us geography and spelling and natural history, looked up at me and went back to the book on his desk. I slumped in my seat, thinking. So that old devil Parsley thought I was going to amount to something! Well, I was determined to do so, and not in the way the superintendent had in mind. But there were deeper thoughts in my brain. Why, I wondered, had I thought with such pleasure of Cora Parsley's pale white shoulder, even imagining I could recall the especial scent it carried that fateful day? Cora was certainly nothing like Standing Alone. She was pretty in a vacant doll-like way, but nothing to appeal to a *Tsistsista*. Of course, I was grateful for her attempt to save me, but how in the world could I—a full-blooded *Tsistsista* and a dedicated man into the bargain—ever consider a white girl as a desirable sexual object? I was so lost in my thoughts I didn't hear Mr. Golightly call my name. My first knowledge he was standing beside my desk was when he rapped me on the head with the pointer he used at the blackboard.

"Dreaming, eh?" he asked, while the class tittered.

"Yes, sir," I mumbled. "I mean—no, sir!"

Beside me Kingfisher had both hands over his mouth in an effort to suppress his giggles.

"After class," Mr. Golightly said, "you will sit here and write one hundred times in your composition book—'I will pay attention in class.' Is that understood, John Beaver?"

"Yes, sir," I said.

Well, I had gotten off easy. But I had not solved the matter of Cora Parsley and my strange feelings. I felt very guilty. Sitting there writing that damned sentence a hundred times, I thought of calling on *Sweet Medicine* for advice. But I decided this was a small matter, after all, that did not warrant bothering him.

As time passed, I did become somewhat educated. Discipline at the school was stern, but the old men were scholars and good teachers. I learned to write English compositions, to keep account books, and more than ever I loved Shakespeare. On many a summer day Cora would meet me in the trees that topped the rise behind the colonel's house. There we would lie in the grass while she read *Hamlet* and *Julius Caesar*, explaining the difficult passages. I knew it was wrong. I knew it was a disgrace to be drawn to such a pale and light-eyed girl. I knew even better that it imperiled my status as a *ho nuh ka wa*. What was I doing, lying in the grass with a white girl? Discovery would imperil my role as a dedicated man—perhaps prevent me from ever accomplishing my mission. Yet I still went willingly—even with anticipation—to these secret meetings.

One day I asked her, "Surely your father doesn't know what you're doing? What would he say if he knew you were up here alone with a Red Indian?"

She had always seemed to me a soft and childlike person. But now she drew herself up with womanly dignity. "I don't care what he would say! My mother died when I was small, and I have kept house for Papa and worked very hard. Now that I am growing up, I have a right to my own way of doing things."

"Nevertheless," I said, "nevertheless—"

Somehow our faces were very close. I do not know exactly how it happened—perhaps I did it, or she did, or we both did—but my mouth was against hers. Only for a fleeting moment, however; she bounded to her feet, looking very queer, and went to arranging her skirt.

"I shall see you again," she said in a trembling voice, "and we—we will read *Measure for Measure*, John Beaver. It is one of my favorites."

I learned a little French, too, and a great deal of Spanish. Manuel Zuniga, the chief cook, was my good friend. I liked the warm smell of the lean-to kitchen where he baked bread and boiled meat. His English was good and he was proud of it, but I coaxed him into speaking only Spanish with me. I picked up languages quickly; soon he and I were chattering in the soft liquid Spanish of Monterrey, where Manuel had a wife and three children. "For," he said, "we are very poor, there in Monterrey, and I had to go away and find a job to make money for my wife and three *niños*, you see?"

"*Sí*," I agreed. "*Por supuesto, es una vida muy dura.*"

We were both exiles. Maybe that strengthened the bond between us.

But with the fascination of all this learning I did not forget my mission. Each night I prayed to *Sweet Medicine*, asking him to put me soon in the way of my enemy. One night, with Kingfisher as lookout, I stole an old Maynard carbine from F Troop. They were going to survey it, anyway, and no one missed it. I didn't know how or when I would be able to use it, but there it was anyway, taken apart, oiled and wrapped in rags and hidden under a loose board in the dormitory. My grandfather had an old carbine, rusty and worn, that he had traded three horses for once, and on my twelfth birthday he had taught me how to shoot. Although Grandfather had little ammunition, he was a good teacher, and in those few shots allowed me I did well. Also, the pony my grandfather gave me to ride back to the Indian Salvation School was still in the post stables, where a kind Irish farrier said he would take care of it for me, though Reverend Parsley insisted it belonged to the government. Somehow I had a romantic idea that soon I would take the stolen rifle, jump on the painted pony, and ride away on a trail of vengeance. I was not sure, however, as to the details.

One day all this was quickly resolved; not

by me, but for me. There was a lot of building activity around Fort McPherson. For some reason the carpenters were building several big sheds down in the meadow, along the river. No one knew what they were for, even the carpenters. But one day they began to build, at the parade ground, something we could identify. It was a reviewing stand.

"Yes," the old farrier said one day when I was in the stables, fondling the nose of my pony, "it's going to be a big event. Fort McPherson, the bigwigs decided, is a very important post all of a sudden. I can't tell you why, because we've been dying on the vine out here for a long time. But General Hazlitt himself is coming next month to—"

"Who?" I blurted.

Garrity looked at me oddly. "Why, General Hazlitt! The big cheese himself! The colonel is laying it on thick for him, hoping some day to be a general himself."

I was stunned, so quickly had the whole thing taken shape right in front of my nose. Hazlitt himself, coming to Fort McPherson! I swallowed hard, my heart suddenly too big for my chest. It was squeezing my inner organs so I couldn't breathe.

"Hey!" Sergeant Garrity called. "John Beaver! What's the matter with you?"

I had already hurried away. Here was my blood

enemy, delivered into my hands! *Sweet Medicine* must have been hard at work all this time, while I wasted my time learning bookkeeping and parsing and the binomial theorem!

CHAPTER SIX

I gathered a tight little band of conspirators, sworn in blood to avenge the grievances of our people by killing the horse soldier Hazlitt when he visited Fort McPherson. Of course I was the leader, being *ho nuh ka wa* from the Medicine Lodge ceremony of the *Tsistsista*. Though the Medicine Lodge was a Cheyenne ceremony, all the boys had similar ceremonies in their tribes, and knew and respected the power of the dedicated man.

So there was I, leader and person agreed on to pull the trigger of the old Maynard carbine. Then there was my good friend Kingfisher; also Bear Louse, Frank Tall Bull, and David Running Bear, who too had been whipped by the superintendent.

Though the sleeping place was locked at night, we managed to hold several meetings. The rest of the boys knew, of course, that something was going on, but not exactly what. After all, when the five of us silently got up and one by one jumped through the window to disappear in the darkness, what were they to think? But I never feared anyone would give us away.

Like a file of *siyuks*—what the white men called ghosts—we flitted through the trees and down the river a mile or more to a jumble of big rocks that made a natural cave. It was beyond the area patrolled by the soldiers; in addition, the noise of the river tumbling over the rocks masked our voices. We could also make a small fire from scraps of wood stolen from the meadow where they were building the mysterious sheds. It was now early spring. Snow lay on the ground, and the night wind was chill. But safe and warm in our refuge, we plotted the horse soldier's death.

"Now," I said, hunkered down over the fire, "we will review my plan. First of all, my own duties. I know them so well I do not have to speak of them again, but I will do so, brothers." In the flickering firelight I looked at their young eager faces, and was proud to be the leader. Grandfather would be proud of me too. "On the morning the horse soldier Hazlitt is to review the troops, there will be no classes, and therefore no roll call of the Indian students. So I leave the dormitory, early in the morning, carrying the pieces of the carbine in my book bag so no one will know what I have in there."

They all nodded. Kingfisher wriggled in excitement.

"I will go to the sutler's store." So that all could see, I held up the key we had made from a wax impression so I could get into the store that holiday morning. "As you all know, the store has a back window overlooking the parade ground. I will go into the storage room, put together the carbine, and watch through the window till the general gets up on the reviewing stand to look at the troops." Although I was certainly not an expert shot, I did not foresee any difficulty in killing Hazlitt from a hundred and fifty yards away, especially when shooting from a rest with carbine propped on the windowsill of the sutler's back room.

I pointed my finger at Kingfisher. "Brother, what do you do?"

Kingfisher was proud of his part. He had stolen some black powder from a broken keg, along with fuse cord, and had made a small bomb which we hoped would be very noisy.

"I sneak away from the place where all the students are standing to watch the ceremonies. Everybody closes up around me so no one sees me leave. Then I go to the hillside in the trees where the bomb is. When I hear the shot from the window, or—"

He hesitated for a moment.

"Well?" I prompted.

"Oh, yes!" His brow cleared. "If the band is playing, I might not hear the music. So I am to watch for the smoke from your shot, or you will wave a hand to signal me!"

"Then?"

He giggled. "I made a very short fuse, and it burns fast, so I will have to get away quick! Anyway, I light it and run away and put my fingers in my ears." Delighted, he grabbed my shoulder. "They never heard such a noise! And that will confuse them and take their eyes and minds away from where they think the shot came from! Oh, such a good plan!"

Modestly I didn't say anything. Though Kingfisher had stolen the powder and made the bomb, *Sweet Medicine* had come to me one night and suggested the idea.

"Very good," I complimented him.

"And I," Bear Louse said, "am to go as soon as I can after the shooting and get the carbine where you will leave it in the big red-flowered bush by the corner of the sheds they are building."

"That's right," I said. Fleeing, I did not want to be hampered by that heavy carbine.

"And I," David Running Bear said, "will take the carbine apart as you, Beaver Killer, showed me, and bury the parts in widely separated places so no one can find them."

Now that the plot was under way, now that my role as puller of the trigger was decided on, I was pleased to see they all called me by my proper Cheyenne name, rather than just "John Beaver."

Frank Tall Bull cleared his throat.

"And you, brother?" I asked.

"In the night," he recited, "I come to you in the hiding place and bring the food stolen from the kitchen, along with the blanket and the knife and the matches and the rest of the stuff."

Pleased, I arose. "I am proud of all of you. The white men will not forget that day. We will avenge our people, the cheated and oppressed and tricked and unjustly slain. We will—"

Kingfisher fidgeted, saying, "Just a minute, brother!"

I was about to embark on a fine speech, one I had gone over many times in my mind, a speech which Grandfather would have been proud to hear, so I was annoyed at Kingfisher.

"Well, what is it?"

He traced circles in the firelit dust with a twig, not looking at me.

"Speak," I ordered.

He looked up. With a queer feeling round my heart I realized how young he seemed. In the long time I had been away Kingfisher had grown, of course, but his face still had some baby roundness, and his eyes were innocent and troubled.

"It is a good plot," he murmured, "and I know it will work, Beaver Killer, because you have planned it. You have a very fine brain, as everybody says. But—"

Uncertainty and doubt are the mortal enemies of any successful conspiracy. As Kingfisher spoke I could feel the strength draining out of our plan, like blood gushing from the steers the soldiers killed every week for meat.

"All right, then," I shouted. "But what? What is troubling you? You act like someone who has seen a *siyuk*!"

"Well," Kingfisher said, "I want you to know, Beaver Killer, that I do not care what happens to me when you kill the general." He swept his arm round to indicate the rest of the band. "I don't think any of us cares! It is a dangerous business, but we all want to strike a blow for our people, and we accepted the danger. But what about the other boys? They are not sworn to anything. They did not take on this job. When it is discovered that you are gone, the soldiers will know you did it. But what if they suspect other Indian students helped you kill the general and helped you get away? It may go bad for the rest of the boys, the ones who were not in the plot. Is that not true?"

For a minute I did not know what to say. It would do no good to shout at him and be angry. He had raised a good point.

"Yes," Bear Louse grumbled, "that has been bothering me too. What do you think about that, Beaver Killer?"

Suddenly I thought of the *parfleche* cylinder hanging round my neck. I took it out, showing it to them. "This is very powerful medicine," I explained. "You all have in your own camps, among your own people, powerful medicines like this. Our best god is *Sweet Medicine*, and he comes to me and tells me what to do when I take out this bit of root in its leather package and pray to him."

They all stared, faces awed.

"Now," I went on, "I am going to ask *Sweet Medicine* whether it is all right for us to go ahead and do what we planned. I am going to ask him whether the plot will come off all right. I am going to ask him if I, Beaver Killer, am alone to accept the blame, or whether others will be punished for what I have done."

I raised my eyes to the night. Overhead a fir bough stirred in the ascending heat from the fire. Bits of burning ash spiraled upward like fireflies, winking out in the darkness overhead. Against the interlocking branches of the trees a sliver of moon peeked through. Somewhere deep in the shadows of the forest an owl hooted, and another called back.

"You, who know all things, have heard me, *Sweet Medicine*," I chanted. "If it is all right with you, please give us a sign everything will come off all right; that the horse soldier Hazlitt will die as planned, and that the blame will fall alone on me, Beaver Killer, grandson of Strong Left Hand, Keeper of your Sacred Arrows!"

Before, whenever I had called on *Sweet Medicine*, I had felt a kind of trembling in my heart when he came near. I was in communion with great dark spirits, and could see a kind of vapor that sprang from the root and spread throughout all space. When he was near I seemed to hang suspended in nothingness, while from that void came the awesome sound of his voice with its measured advice. This time, however, nothing happened. Was *Sweet Medicine* listening to me? I did not get that well-remembered feeling. Was he turning his face away from me?

"*Sweet Medicine!*" I called, louder this time. I held the cylinder high in the firelight. "Come down to us, talk to us, give us your blessing!"

Kingfisher, I saw from the corner of my eye, was getting restless. He opened his mouth as if to say something. Desperate, I shuffled round the fire in a slow dance, waving the cylinder and chanting.

"Now is when we need you, *Sweet Medicine*! Come down to us and speak!"

It was no good. *Sweet Medicine* was busy someplace else, or maybe he was turning his face away. It was a fact that I did not have the sacred feeling. I felt ordinary, and very foolish. *Sweet Medicine*, my guide in all things, had not come to me.

"Well?" Kingfisher demanded.

What could I say? After going so far, was

this a sign that I should give up my plan? Had something gone wrong that *Sweet Medicine* saw from on high, and so withheld his final approval?

"What did *Sweet Medicine* say?" Frank Tall Bull asked.

Bear Louse was an Arapaho, and they are very suspicious, not trusting anybody. "Or," Bear Louse asked, "did he say anything? Tell us, brother!"

I set my teeth hard together. No matter what *Sweet Medicine* said or did, I would not give up. This was too important to the *Tsistsista.* If I suffered for it, then I was ready. If my band of conspirators suffered for it, they knew the danger when they joined. And if the rest of the boys, the ones not in on the plot, suffered for it—why, that was all right! They were Indians, too. Their people all had suffered under the white man's heel. Why should they not take their share of the consequences?

"Yes," I cried. "Of course, he spoke to me, as he always does!" I hesitated, finding words hard to form. I was not used to lying. "He—he came to me, in my heart—" I slapped a fist against my chest. "In here he came to me! He said—he said everything would be all right, not to worry. That was what he said."

Kingfisher's eyes were wide and dark; the fire shone in them. I think he believed me. But Bear Louse and Frank Tall Bull looked doubtful.

"I wonder," Bear Louse muttered, "if you are telling the truth, John Beaver. I always know when spirits are around, and it did not seem to me anything special happened."

"I don't believe you, either," Frank Tall Bull sniffed. "I think you are just saying that."

Kingfisher spoke up angrily. "Beaver Killer does not lie! I have never known him to lie!"

David Running Bear scratched his nose, and looked into the fire. "Well, maybe this plan is not such a good idea after all," he said. "Maybe—"

They all broke off chattering in sudden alarm. Something huge and gray caromed into the firelight, reeling this way and that. It was one of the great horned owls of the forest, and it swooped down near the flames, raising a cloud of sparks and ashes, wings beating powerfully so we felt the rush of air against our cheeks. Almost as quickly as it came, it disappeared again into the night. All that was left to mark its passing was a cloud of fine white ash and a suddenly renewed flame. That, and a downy feather that floated on the rising heat till Kingfisher jumped up and snatched it.

"There!" he shouted. "Look at that! It is a sign from *Sweet Medicine* himself, just like Beaver Killer promised! What more could you want? I *told* you my brother does not lie!"

They all shrank back in great respect, and made sacred signs. *Sweet Medicine* had been here, they believed. Everything would come out all right.

"I am sorry I said what I did," Bear Louse muttered.

"Me, too," Frank Tall Bull agreed, backing uneasily away from me.

"It is a good sign," David Running Bear said. "A very good sign, brother! We want you to know we are all with you, and will do our parts well."

When the meeting broke up, Kingfisher saw me sitting next to the fire, gazing into it, and asked, "Aren't you coming back to the dormitory now?" He pointed to the east where a glimmer of light showed along the sawlike-edge of the mountains. "The hour is late!"

"No," I said. "I—I want to sit here a little while and do some more thinking. Later I will come."

"All right," Bear Louse warned, "but remember some soldiers may be up early and catch you. Be careful!"

I sat for a long time looking into the dying embers of the fire. Great owl or no, *Sweet Medicine* had *not* come that night. It had been an accident; an owl, pursuing some small night-bird, had blundered into the circle of firelight. Blinded, it had fallen into the fire, and then soared away with a powerful beat of its wings, leaving behind a scorched feather. It was no message from *Sweet Medicine*, though the rest of the boys believed so. It was just an accident. Maybe a lucky accident,

118

maybe (depending on the way things turned out) an unlucky one.

Either way I was committed. Feeling very tired, I got to my feet, scuffing dirt over the embers, and walked back toward the meadow. It was hard to be a dedicated man. *Ohohyaa*!

It was difficult to get information about when General Hazlitt would visit Fort McPherson; especially hard without seeming to be too interested in it, and thus giving away our plan. But David Running Bear picked up pennies blacking boots for the troopers, and I sometimes hung around the stables; Bear Louse helped out at the sutler's store, and Frank Tall Bull was a favorite of Emma White, the adjutant's housekeeper, and overheard bits of gossip from her. So, though the various stories we heard were contradictory and confusing, by putting them all together it seemed likely General Hazlitt would be at the post early in May.

The weeks dragged by. Now that we had the whole thing planned, and so well planned at that, we wanted to put it into effect. Boys our age do not gladly wait for anything. Most of all I was afraid that my little band would lose interest in the scheme and grow dull and listless while they waited. So it was up to me to keep them going. Even though all details had been settled, I still had them meet at the customary place.

Our repeated night excursions made it likely we would soon be discovered and the plot ruined, but it was a risk I had to take.

Bear Louse was the worst. He kept complaining, and saying, "Why do we have to meet so often? What reason is there to keep getting up in the middle of the night?"

Frank Tall Bull yawned, stretching his arms high. "That is right! I go to sleep in class any more, and Mr. Golightly keeps smacking me with his pointer. I tell you, someone is going to get suspicious pretty soon! Then we will all be in a fix!"

As best I could I soothed them. I seemed to have some of my grandfather's skill as an orator, and I told them long stories about the *Tsistsista* and all the times the white men had treated us bad, pointing out too how their own people had suffered. For a while it worked pretty well; I could get them worked to fever pitch, anxious to strike when the time came. But after a while even that didn't work. They got to arguing with me when I tried to wake them for another midnight meeting. As I have said, it is hard to be a leader.

But late in April, only a few days before General Hazlitt was coming to Fort McPherson, something happened that changed all that. And it was a great shock to me, I can tell you that. I was working in the kitchen with my friend Zuniga, learning how to cut up a rancid side of beef that was too much even for the soldiers to eat (that was why the school got it). By this time my Spanish was pretty good; Manuel himself said so. Now he was intent on teaching me the *modismos*, the funny little ways of saying things that languages have; that is to say, the way a soldier from F Troop might tell someone, "I had to light a shuck out of there." He didn't really light anything, and I didn't know what a shuck was, but of course it meant he had to hurry away from someplace.

"*Pues*," Zuniga said, "*tenemos modismos en Español, también.* Spanish has got more *modismos* than any language, you bet. Like 'to take a walk.' In Spanish you don't take a walk, my friend John Beaver. You '*darme un paseo*'— you *give* yourself a walk. Sound funny, eh? But not in Spanish. It is a nice expression."

I was thinking that over when Kingfisher rushed up to the kitchen, round-eyed and excited.

"John Beaver!" he called. "The superintendent wants to see you in his office! Come quick!"

Kingfisher and I stared for a moment at each other. I know we were each thinking the same thing. Had the plot been discovered? I stood there so long, the stinking cleaver dangling from my hand, that Zuniga said, "Better go along, boy. That man, he don't like to be keep waiting."

"All right," I said. "*Voy a darme un paseo*, I guess."

121

Silently the two of us walked back to Reverend Parsley's house. I wiped my hands on the bloody apron I was wearing and gave it to Kingfisher to take back to the kitchen. Then I knocked at the door.

Cora let me in. She looked frightened. *Ohohyaa*! Very bad! Maybe it was something else. Maybe the superintendent had found out Cora and I were—were—

"Papa is waiting for you," she whispered, one hand at her throat, very pale. "You are to go on right up, John Beaver."

When I knocked at the door of the study, Reverend Parsley called, "Come in."

Slowly I opened the door. This was very bad. At his desk sat the superintendent, looking gloomy. In a big leather chair next to the globe sat Captain Germany, the regimental adjutant, swinging one skinny booted leg over the arm of the chair and twisting his mustache with his fingers. In a straight-backed chair sat a man I had never seen before; a red-faced man in a flowered vest with a gold watch chain, a black bowler hat in his lap. Scanty black hair was combed across his dome, and even from the doorway I could smell pomade.

"Come over here, by the window," the superintendent said, "where we can see you and talk to you, John Beaver."

When I did, Reverend Parsley cleared his

throat, looking stern and sad. "You have been called here," he said, "to explain how——"

"Just a minute," Captain Germany interrupted. "Dammit, Parsley, this is an Army matter! Let me start the proceedings."

Well, it wasn't my visits with Cora, then. That could hardly be an Army matter. But that knowledge only made my burden heavier. They had discovered the plot, and probably the Maynard carbine, and the parts of Kingfisher's bomb, and all the rest. I was so scared I felt I must make water, right then and there, on the floor in the sight of them and *Sweet Medicine* and *Heammawihio* and everybody. Too, my manhood seemed to be retreating far up into my bowels.

"Sit down, son," Captain Germany said, indicating a chair.

I did so, grateful for the support.

"Thank you, sir," I said.

Germany jerked his head at the red-faced man. "This fellow here——" Something in the way he said it sounded scornful. "Mr. Laban Perkins is a detective—a Pinkerton man, from back East."

When I ran my tongue round my lips, they seemed dry; my tongue stuck like it was going across an old board. Down below some of the Indian School boys were trimming trees under the direction of one of the teachers, and burning twigs and branches. A shred of the acrid smoke came into the room and then drifted out again.

"I'll be brief," Captain Germany said. "There used to be a trapper come into the post and get drunk once in a while—raise a rookus and try to rape all the laundresses and such. Jake Noggle. A rascal, believe me!"

The Pinkerton man looked indignant, but the adjutant waved a hand to shut him up.

"Well, every dog's got a family somewhere, I suppose. Jake had a rich one, back in Boston, so this man tells me. And when they didn't hear from Jake in a month of Sundays, they made inquiries."

My heart sank. Noggle! The bearded sot I had killed, the one who caught me with his goats and tried to make a woman out of me the time I fled from the school! But that had been almost two years ago!

"No one saw Jake for a long time," Captain Germany went on. "Someone thought he had a diggings of some sort up in the Iron Mountains, but no one was sure. Well, mail went back and forth, and finally—"

"Finally," Mr. Perkins broke in, "the family hired me to investigate."

The adjutant gave him a grim look. "It seems Perkins found Noggle's hideout. Only Noggle wasn't there. At least not in the flesh. All that was left was moldering bones. But from the hacked condition of the skull, and from a bloody ax Perkins found near the cabin, it appears old Jake

Noggle was done in." Captain Germany held his nose with his fingers, and blew hard. Then he leaned back in his chair, looking satisfied. "And good riddance to a scoundrel, I say!"

Perkins was indignant. "Noggle came from a very good family," he protested. "Maybe he was a kind of black sheep, but his family has a great deal of money. They hired me to undertake the case, and I don't think it's Christian to speak ill of the deceased!"

I tried to swallow, but nothing would go down my throat. Did they know anything? How could they connect me with Noggle's death?

Captain Germany's eyebrows bristled. "I'll speak any way I goddam want!" he said to the Pinkerton man. "This is an Army matter, and the Army has jurisdiction!" When the detective turned red and didn't say anything, the adjutant went on. "Show him what you have there, Perkins."

I hadn't seen the paper-wrapped parcel under the chair, but Mr. Perkins drew it out and pulled off the paper. It was an old Hudson's Bay blanket, once red, but now stained and torn and full of holes.

"When you ran away," the adjutant said, "I remember Emma White, my housekeeper, had given you a red blanket, one of my own personal blankets, not Army issue." He showed me a monogram stitched into a corner. "Detective

Perkins found this blanket not too far from Noggle's camp."

The blanket! The red blanket! After I had slain Noggle, I wandered toward my grandfather's camp. As in a dream I remembered throwing that blanket away when I became sick and feverish in the snow.

"It is possible," Captain Germany said, "or at least Detective Perkins thinks it possible, that you were fleeing to your grandfather's camp in the Iron Mountains. Since you ran away with no supplies, no gun, no knife, no food, he suspects you came on Noggle's camp and killed him for the things you needed to continue your journey."

My head swam. I was so surrounded with snares I didn't dare make a move. Admitting killing Jake Noggle, even if he was a scoundrel, would send me to jail. And right now, even if I denied it, there would still be suspicion that might give away the plot to kill General Hazlitt. What a bear trap was yawning at my feet!

"Come, come!" the adjutant urged. "Out with it, boy! Did you kill Noggle with the ax?"

I couldn't say anything. My tongue seemed stuck fast to the roof of my mouth, and my hands tightened on the edge of the chair until I thought I would break it.

"He's guilty," Mr. Perkins said with satisfaction. "Oh, I seen a many of 'em! When they're confronted with the deed, they always clams up."

For the first time Reverend Parsley spoke. He ran a nervous hand through his white hair, saying, "John Beaver, this is a serious charge. Speak, boy, and save yourself if you can!"

I bowed my head and stared at the floor.

"Well," Perkins said, "I'm satisfied." He reached in his pocket and came out with a pair of manacles. "I'll just take him along and—"

"You won't do any such goddam thing," Captain Germany said.

"What?"

"You heard me."

Perkins's red face got redder. "But—"

"But me no goddam buts," the adjutant said. He got up and came to pull me up from the chair by the arm. "This boy is a ward of the Army. You can't lay a hand on him till you go to someplace like Cheyenne and get a Federal warrant. In the meantime, I want to talk to him—alone, and at my leisure, without any goddam hired bloodhounds around."

Mr. Laban Perkins protested. "But he's a prime suspect, captain!"

Reverend Parsley was worried, too. "John Beaver could be dangerous! At least, captain, put him in the guardhouse till Mr. Perkins can get the necessary papers!"

The adjutant's hand on my shoulder helped still my trembling. I felt strength flow into my legs, and my pounding heart slowed. I was saved, at least for a while—and I had admitted nothing.

"The guardhouse," Captain Germany said, "is filled with sodomites, murderers, and goddam blasphemers. No, I'll keep him in my own little jail till we get a few things straightened out. Anyway, I don't think you've got much of a case against him." He nodded curtly to the two others, and marched me out into the setting sun of a spring afternoon. For safekeeping he had Sergeant Garrity, the farrier, lock me in the feed room of the stables. As the sun rose the next morning, I turned sixteen years old.

CHAPTER SEVEN

It turned out I was going to *darme un paseo*—to take a walk, as Zuniga translated it—but I didn't realize what a long walk it would be, and how long a time would pass before I saw my people again.

For three days I stayed locked in the feed room. It was almost May, and the smell of the outside was more than I could bear. There is a scent to spring that makes the body tremble with delight, a smell that is better than any white woman's perfume, because it goes deep inside you and is as if *Heammawihio* himself touched you with his hand. So I sighed, and was sad, and Sergeant Garrity said I groaned a lot in my sleep. He was

128

concerned. Being a kind man, for a soldier, he said so.

"Now don't you worry, sonny! Everything's going to come out fine! They ain't really got anything against you; the adjutant hisself said so."

He mistook my emotions. If they could prove I had killed Jake Noggle, then I would probably die. That was all right; a lot of the *Tsistsista* had died, facing the prospect with courage. So would I when the time arrived. But my unease came from a different source. It was spring, the birds talked among themselves outside my barred window, and my loins ached. I thought desperately of Standing Alone, the brown flash of her thighs as she kicked the ball at *oassiof*. Treacherously, but unable to help myself, I dreamed also of Cora Parsley and her warm soft body beside me as she read from the Sonnets. It was spring, and spring is a hard time for a young man, no matter whether he is in jail or not.

I suppose it was not so bad. Sergeant Garrity brought me hot food from the troopers' mess, and sat for long hours outside the slatted wooden door trying to cheer me up. But he was also very careful, never giving me a chance to escape. "For," he said, "you're my responsibility, John Beaver. If you was to get away, Captain Germany would have my balls, and that's a fact! So I'll just check this lock—" He rattled the rusty chain.

"Good night to you, sonny. Sleep peaceful, eh?"

Garrity dozed on a straw pallet atop a pile of feed sacks near my door, single-action Army Colt at hand. If other things didn't keep me awake, his snoring did. The sky turned silver, then gold; a yellow moon slid up the heavens, and a shaft of light brightened my dusty oat-smelling prison. From a long way off I heard a coyote bay the moon; first one, then another, then a lot of them, so the night was filled with tremolos.

Arms locked around my knees, I stared at the patch of light on the dirt floor, watching it creep by my feet like the hands of a clock. It was quiet, except for the dwindling complaints of the coyotes; the hour was well after midnight. But there was another sound, too, under the wailing of my coyote brothers. I listened hard. It was a scratching noise, as a small animal might make in digging through to the sacks of corn and oats.

A rat, I decided. Well, a rat had a right to eat, too. I wished him luck, and put my head on my knees, trying to sleep. But the noise went on, becoming louder and louder. From time to time it stopped, then resumed.

If it was a rat, it was a big one. Then, incredibly, I heard the whisper of voices. They came from far away, faint and muffled. Rats did not speak words. I knelt down, pressing my ear against the hard-packed earth. Whose voices? And where?

The digging sounds became louder. Now I

could hear the metallic sound of a shovel or a spade as it bit into the earth beneath me. Someone was digging into my prison! Was I to be rescued? Pressing my ear harder against the earth, I heard a giggle. Kingfisher and my friends were there, digging their way like moles into my cell!

Fearfully I looked toward the piled feed sacks where Garrity was sleeping. There was no sound except a bubbling kind of gargle. Just then something gave under my knees, and I sank slowly into a hole that seemed to open under me. I subsided into a kind of stew composed of legs, arms, shovels, loose dirt, a few rocks, and whispering, excited voices—all lit by the rays of a coal-oil lantern which was quickly extinguished, when my rescuers learned that they had at last broken through.

"John Beaver!" a voice hissed in my ear. "Is that you?"

I gripped Kingfisher's arm hard.

"It is me, all right! Oh, what a dangerous thing to do! But I am glad you are here! I could not stand being in this jail much longer!"

Now we could see each other in the moonlight. Putting a finger to my lips I gestured toward the sleeping Garrity. Kingfisher nodded. The rest clustered round naked, except for underdrawers, smelling of earth and sweat. I saw Frank Tall Bull and David Running Bear and others, and gripped their muddy hands in thanks.

"We must move fast," Kingfisher warned. "John Beaver, you've got to be a long way from here when the soldiers wake up and find you gone."

"But where will I go?" I asked.

Now it was my friend Kingfisher who was the planner, the wise man in the council, the giggling little boy who had grown up. He made me feel foolish.

"That is for you to say," he grunted. "With your light skin and eyes and the smart head on your shoulders, you will get along." He jerked his head toward the window. "We stole your pony, and it is outside there, with food and a gun we stole also. There are blankets and water and cartridges and everything you need. Hurry, now, before Garrity wakes up."

Almost as if he heard us, Garrity groaned in his sleep, rolled over, sniffling and wheezing, then settled back among the grain sacks.

"Wait a minute," I said. "What about General Hazlitt?"

Kingfisher, waist-deep in the yawning hole, pulled at my arm. "Come on!"

"Not yet," I complained, drawing my arm away. "I have sworn to kill that man when he comes here! What about our plan, and the arrangements we made?"

Kingfisher sighed. He said something down into the hole, where the others had vanished, and climbed back out. "Listen," he said. "Listen, brother. We will take care of that! It is too dangerous for you to stay around here any more. Besides, we hear they may take you away to Cheyenne or someplace to stand trial. So you have to run away. But we will take care of the horse soldier Hazlitt. We still have the carbine and the bullets and all the rest, and we will kill him as we planned. I will take *your* place, friend. It is all arranged. Now we must go!"

Still I pulled away from him. "No," I said angrily. "No, you can not do that! You will all be in enough trouble if they discover you dug me out of this place. Besides, to kill Hazlitt is *my* job! I do not let even a good friend like you do this thing for me. It is my job, I have sworn to do it, and I will do it."

Kingfisher was puzzled. "But how—"

"Don't worry," I said. "There will be other chances for me. Wherever Hazlitt goes, I will follow him. Some day, maybe a long way and a long time from here, I will catch up with him again. Then I will kill him, as I swore to my grandfather and to the *Tsistsista!*"

Kingfisher was unhappy. He hit himself on the bare chest with his fist, and said, "We drew lots, and the gods picked *me* to do it! I can not help it if you must go away, John Beaver! But when you go away, then someone has to avenge the people! And I—"

I grabbed his arm so hard he winced. "Shut

133

up!" I hissed. "You are still a child, brother! Never interfere in what is between a man and *Heammawihio*! This was decided a long time ago in our tribe. I was born to avenge our people, and I live to avenge them! After all, your people were not on the Washita where this great shame came on us! There were no Sioux there! This is *my* job, and I will call a curse on you if you try to meddle!"

Kingfisher shrank back, slowly lowering his eyes. My passion frightened him. "All right," he said sulkily.

"You will not interfere? You will get rid of that old carbine and forget the plan? Leave Hazlitt to me?"

"All right. I guess so."

"Swear it!"

He hesitated.

"Swear it!" I insisted.

Resignedly he pointed overhead, then down to the earth. "I swear by the Great Spirit and by the Mother Earth."

That was pretty good, because an oath made like that binds not only a man's own tribe, but all the people. I was not satisfied, however; I had to make sure. Remembering some of the Sioux things Kingfisher had told me, I reached for the shovel. In the moonlight the edge of the blade sparkled where the digging had worn and polished it.

"Kiss this," I said.

"What?"

"Do as I told you!"

When making an important oath, the Sioux kiss a knife or an arrowhead or other sharp instrument. This means if they are false to the oath, death will come by the sharp instrument they have touched with their lips. I had no knife or arrowhead; the shovel would have to do.

"Hurry!" I muttered. "We have to go!"

Angrily Kingfisher bent and kissed the polished blade. It made him mad, but I knew he would always keep that oath.

I still didn't know where to go, except away— away from Fort McPherson and the Indian Salvation School and the Pinkerton detective. So I rode and rode through the night. By the time the sun rose I was far upstream on the White River, the one that flowed through Fort McPherson, flogging the paint pony and looking over my shoulder for signs of pursuit.

It rained that night, a gentle warm rain. I spent a few hours before dawn huddled among the roots of a great oak tree, chewing on a cake of mush and some cold fried pork my friends had packed in the saddlebags. As the sky became pink with dawn, the pony turned sad eyes toward me. I had ridden him hard; peeling scabs of dried foam still showed on his flanks. When I whistled he came, but without interest. Shambling over to me, he stood quietly as I tightened the cinch under his belly.

"Brother," I said, "I am sorry to use you so hard. But there is a long way to go."

All that day we scrambled through rising slopes littered with a gray shale that cut the pony's fetlocks, making him scramble and sometimes fall to his knees. Rocks reflected the heat of the sun in my face so that I sweated hard, and clouds of stinging gnats gathered round my head. The pony's tongue hung out, limp and lolling, and his sides wheezed so they lifted my legs out and back, out and back, as he panted for breath. But at last we topped a shallow pass into a wooded bowl, and I flung myself gratefully down in a bed of brown pine needles, falling into a deep sleep.

It was afternoon the next day when I woke. Panicky, I jumped to my feet, fearing that while I had slept my pursuers must certainly have come upon me. But when I searched the rocky pass above, I saw nothing but the failing rays of the sun lighting the rubble with a slanting glow. Even as I watched the shaft of sunlight crept up and up, and finally the pass was left in gloom. The sun had set.

Next morning the pony's feet were so cut and sore I had to lead him. I didn't know how far we were from Fort McPherson, but it was not far enough. On we blundered through scrubby brush and stunted trees, myself pulling the pony forward and he lagging back, so that in the whole morning we covered not more than two or three miles. At noon I think I was more tired than the pony, but I had given his sore hoofs a rest, and by evening he perked up a little.

That pony was tougher than I was. When I awoke I didn't know whether I could get up or not. My joints ached, my head hurt, my feet were sore, my stomach felt as if it were full of worms writhing and twisting. The flight had told on me; the physical effort, the fear of pursuit, the worry over whether Kingfisher and the rest had gotten into trouble over my escape. But this morning the pony came to me almost friskily, giving me a playful nip as I hoisted the saddle on him.

"Brother," I said, "do not have fun with me. It is too early in the morning, and I do not feel well."

Fortunately, however, my spirits improved during the day. The way became easier, and now, I thought, we must be far ahead of any pursuit. In a very gradual way, I began to relax a little, even to enjoy myself.

In a noonday stop I bent over a shallow basin in an outcropping of rock, now filled with rain. After sucking up deep draughts of the cool water, I sat for a moment hunched on my heels, staring down at the figure reflected from the silent pool.

Haggard eyes stared back at me. The being in the pool had a straggle of black hairs on upper lip and chin, and I brushed at them with the back of my hand. Hair on the face the *Tsistsista* considered brutish; bears and white men had hair on the face, and my grandfather and the other men of our tribe kept it plucked out with clamshell tweezers.

The creature of the pool was young, perhaps, but heavily weighed down with responsibility. Thin, he was, and tall; as I backed away from the pool I saw him lengthen and lengthen, finally disappearing as I straightened up. Would he pass in the white man's world for—perhaps for a Mexican? Fingering my torn and threadbare clothes, I wondered.

In this Moon When the Horses Get Fat the weather was very good. The river was high from the spring rains, and water tumbled through the rocks in a noisy spray; the new leaves of the willows were dark green, and sparkled with diamonds of fiery water. Now I rode across a sunlit grassy plain. Heavy belts of forest covered the mountains below the snowline, and the green of their boughs came down the foothills well into the plain below. With pleasure I heard the song of meadowlarks, the chirping of thousands of grasshoppers. Everything smelled fresh and clean and promising, and after a while I began to sing myself. I sang the song of the kit-fox, our brother *Si No Pah*, because I remembered my grandfather's words; *you must be like Si No Pah, wise and cunning yet very quick.* The words went like this:

> "My friends,
> Nothing lives long
> Except the rocks!"

In honor of the spring, I sang the Willow Dance Song, then some of the wolf-songs young men sing when they go out to seek the enemy and establish a reputation. That was what I was doing, too. Ambling through the meadow, stopping once in a while to let the painted pony graze on the new grass, I felt strong and powerful. Youth rose in me like the sap of the trees, and flowed into all parts of my body. I remembered my grandfather's song of the *Mahuts*, the Sacred Arrows; I sang that too:

> "My weapon I use,
> Skin of rattlesnake,
> Skin of bull-snake,
> I use the water-snake."

I felt a little uneasy singing that song, remembering it was very sacred and to be sung only by the Keeper of the Arrows himself. But I was *ho nuh ka wa*, and perhaps that made it all right.

Besides, was I not on intimate terms with the gods? *Sweet Medicine* himself had looked down on me the night I tried to get his approval of the plot to kill Hazlitt. Then he deliberately stayed up there to sign the plot would fail. Obviously, he knew the Pinkerton man was after me. So he was watching over me and everything would be all right.

Still singing, I topped a grassy rise sprinkled with wildflowers. In the distance was a house of sawed lumber with a fence around it. There were large outbuildings, too, and a lot of horses in pens.

I sat there a long time, looking at the buildings. The pony became impatient to go on, and made a few little dancing steps. I sawed hard on the reins, making him stand still so I could think. Should I swing around to the north, toward the pass in the mountains? No, it was cold up there, with snow. But to the south was the river, now too deep and icy to swim across.

The pony swung his head and tried to nip my knee. It was his way of saying, "Let's be off!" I was still undecided, but then the throught came to me. Sooner or later I would have to face the white people. Sooner or later I would have to go among them, pretending I was one of them instead of a Cheyenne young man anxious to avenge his people. That morning I felt invincible. So what better time than now? I kneed the pony;

he sprang across the high grass, stirring a cloud of buzzing crickets.

As I rode, I went over in my mind my new identity. I would be—well, Mexican would be a good choice. With knowledge of the language, and the fact that I was a long way from Manuel Zuniga's Monterrey, I could probably get by. The buildings grew larger and I could make out individual horses in the pens. *Wise and cunning, yet very quick.* Of course I spoke English well, too, my mother having been a—perhaps a Texan lady.

When I saw the little group in the grove of trees near the house, I reined up, frightened in spite of myself. It had been one thing to talk about going among the white people, but another to do it. But the sight of them came on me so quickly I could not turn back. Slowly I rode toward the grove, taking my hat off and holding it in my hand.

"Hello!" I called, not knowing what else to say.

There were several of them; some rough-looking men with shovels, a sad-faced man, lean and stringy, with a drooping mustache, and a queenly woman in black who sat in a wagon, holding the reins in her hand. There was also a rough pine box; the men were digging a grave. They looked at me without interest, then went on digging. The stringy man nodded, then went back to looking into the hole. But the woman smiled, and waved a ring-covered hand.

"Good morning, young man," she called back.

That was how I met Orlo Pratt and Madam Blanche, his wife. That was how I came to Orlo Pratt's horse ranch. That is how I came to know about a lot of things I was pretty late in finding out.

I do not want to dwell on the Pratts and their Slash Dollar ranch too much, because sometimes I am ashamed of what happened there. Again, maybe it was all right. Perhaps it was time for it to happen. If it had not happened there, it might have come about elsewhere under bad circumstances. Anyway, it happened, and this is the way it was.

The man they were burying was the Chinese cook. Sam Fat had been on the Slash Dollar for a long time, and finally died because he was eighty-two or ninety-two years old—he himself did not know exactly. Accepting my story, the Pratts took me in and fed me, letting me sleep in the bunkhouse with the men. The hands were more reserved, sometimes looking at me strangely and muttering among themselves. One of them, a lanky sunburned man named Red Gulick, seemed particularly to dislike me. Once, when I came into the bunkhouse where they were playing cards, I heard Red say, "Why, here comes the pretty boy!" and they all guffawed. But when I gave them a fierce look, they only shrugged and laughed and went back to their cards.

My stay in the bunkhouse didn't last long, however. When I told Mr. Orlo Pratt I would like to stay on at the Slash Dollar, he asked me what I could do.

"Well," I said, "I'm a good hand with horses."

He shook his head. "Don't need no wranglers. Got more lazy saddle bums around here than I need."

I remembered Sam Fat, and said, "I can cook."

For the past few days, one of the hands had been cooking, and it tasted awful. Madam Pratt wouldn't eat it at all, and was living on canned things from Denver.

"Cook?" Mr. Pratt demanded. "Did you say you could cook?"

From then on I was Juan Castor, the cook. It was my own little joke, that Juan Castor. In Spanish it meant "John Beaver." You pronounced it with the Castor accented hard on the last syllable. Though I had a little trouble at first, I finally became a pretty good cook, what with the experience I had from Manuel Zuniga. No one questioned my Mexican blood, though one of the hands was a Mexican named Agustin. He and I talked a little in Spanish once and he thought my accent sounded *un poco extraño*—a little strange— but nothing came of it. So I began to feel pretty good, and thought about planning my next move.

I liked Mr. Pratt. His wife ruled the place, that was easy to see, and sad-faced Mr. Pratt worked hard to make the money so she could have the things she wanted; fine furniture, the latest Eastern fashions, diamonds for her fingers and bosom, a Scandinavian housekeeper who bustled about the house, washing windows and dusting, and lived somewhere up under the eaves of the big house. One day, in the pause between dinner and supper, I walked into the little shed where Mr. Pratt had his office. He and the hands were out on the range, and I leafed idly through his account books. At the school I had learned to keep books, and was curious how a real set of ledgers looked.

I was astounded how much money Mr. Pratt made selling horses. Slash Dollar horses went to Cheyenne City, to North Platte, even back to Omaha on the Union Pacific Railroad. I even found some old bills of lading tucked into the books where they shipped horses to Fort McPherson. And while I was pondering that, I found papers for one batch shipped years ago to Fort Lincoln, near Omaha, receipted for by W. E. Hazlitt, Lieutenant Colonel, USA. That made my blood tingle, I can tell you.

The books were not current, I could see that. Maybe Mr. Pratt did his own books, and had been too busy to keep them up. Or maybe he had had a bookkeeper—some of the entries were in a different and very ornate hand—and had lost him. I wondered.

When Mrs. Orlo Pratt would go to Cheyenne City once a month, she would bring me back shirts and pants and things I needed. She was beautiful, and very kind to me, and I complimented myself on how well I was doing in this strange new world. Though never forgetting my mission, I began to enjoy the white man's life. *Quick and cunning,* I remembered; that was it, but there was no reason I should not enjoy myself in this meantime.

Cooking soon got to be a dull and wearisome job. The hands wolfed down in minutes the food I took hours to prepare, and then there was the different and special cooking I had to do for Madam Pratt. She was always bringing me special recipes. "For you know, Juanito," she said, "I have a delicate stomach, and must eat only the light and easily digestible foods."

One day, weary of the stench of boiled beef and beans that permeated the kitchen, I jerked off my apron and went out for a breath of fresh air. Mr. Pratt was sitting in the office, biting a stub of pencil.

"Sir," I said.

He swiveled round, still chewing on the pencil. "Oh, it's you, Juan Castor.

"What do you want?"

"Well," I said, "I'm dissatisfied with being a cook."

He had been paying me ten dollars a month

and food, but now he didn't bat an eyelash. "Fifteen dollars a month," he said. "How does that sound?"

I shook my head. "It isn't the money. It's just that I—" I gestured toward the books. "Anyone can cook. But I can keep books for you. I noticed they weren't up to date, and I found some errors, too."

His sad face got even sadder. "You been goin' through my books, boy? Now who in hell give you permission?"

"Please, sir," I blurted out. "I didn't think I was doing anything wrong! I—I was just tired of the kitchen, and when I saw the books it reminded me how I used to do it, and I used to *like* it, too, in a way, and so I sat here and looked through them. But I didn't mean anything wrong."

He sat there a long time, pulling at his drooping mustaches. Finally he threw the pencil stub down and said, "Keep books, eh? And cook? Seems to me you're a kid with quite some education, to be wandering round this country. What else do you do?"

"Well," I said, "I'm a fair hand with animals, too, but that's beside the point. I've looked at your books, and no one appears to be doing right by them, so I thought I'd like to help out."

I didn't discover till later that the previous bookkeeper, a man named Vernon Boxheimer,

146

had been fired for paying too much attention to Mrs. Pratt. At least that was the gossip in the bunkhouse.

"Look here," Mr. Pratt said. "The bookkeeper on a ranch like the Slash Dollar is an important man, and a likely one is hard to come by. I've had ads in the Denver papers for three months, and I ain't located one yet. You sure you ain't bitin' off more 'n you can chew, boy?"

"I can do it," I said.

"Well—" He got up, pacing about the tiny shed, gnarled hands locked behind his back. Finally he stopped and looked at me. "God knows," he said, "I been rackin' my brain the last three months tryin' to figure out if we're makin' or losin' money. If you can straighten out those books, boy, I'll hire you. And if you *keep* 'em straightened out, there's twenty dollars a month goes with the job!"

As I hurried away, elated, he called me back.

"There's one thing I ought to tell you," he said. "I had some trouble with my last bookkeeper."

"He wrote a very fine hand," I said.

He looked hard at me, chewing on his mustache. "Yes," he said, "he did. But the trouble was—" He broke off, and his face worked. He seemed very agitated. Finally he shook his head, and waved me away. "Go 'long with you, boy," he said. " 'Twan't nothin'. I guess my brains is just gettin' soft, that's all."

I got the books back in shape; it wasn't very hard. And I discovered why Mr. Pratt had such a time with them. He could hardly read and write, but was too proud to say so. But he hired a new cook from Cheyenne City, and I had full time to devote to the books. I don't know who was prouder of my accomplishment; Mr. Pratt or me.

At Madam Blanche's insistence I had my own room, a cubbyhole in a corner of the house high up under the eaves. Life was very fine, except for those anxious moments when I thought about Grandfather and my people, especially Kingfisher and Bear Louse and the rest of my friends at Fort McPherson. Had they escaped punishment for my flight? Indeed, had General Hazlitt ever come to Fort McPherson as had been planned? I pored over old copies of the Denver *Post*, searching for news. But there was none.

One day I was sitting in the little office shed, casting up accounts, when I felt someone nearby looking over my shoulder.

"Oh, there you are!" Madam Blanche said.

Quickly I stood up.

"Yes, ma'am," I said.

Mr. Orlo Pratt was out on the range, roping horses for a big shipment to the Mormons in Salt Lake City. No one else was around.

"I see you are busy," she smiled. "You are always so busy! Orlo tells me you are the hardest-working man on the Slash Dollar. He doesn't know what he'd do without you."

She was a majestic woman, always dressed in black, with brassy hair piled high on her head and held in place by a set of jeweled combs. I never learned how to judge the age of white people, but I thought Mr. Pratt was about fifty. So I would judge Madam Blanche to be thirty-five or so. At any rate, her complexion was flawless; pale and velvety, and the eyes were soft and brown, with sunny glints in them.

"That's—that's nice of him," I stammered.

She took my arm, pulling me out into the summer sunshine. "All work and no play—" she laughed. "Come along with me, Juanito; see what I have for you."

Silently I trailed her across the lawn to the front porch, hearing the *swish-swish-swish* of her skirt as it brushed the grass. The house was silent. I followed her like a *siyuk* through the elegant drawing room with its crystal mirrors and brocade sofas, the carved wood stands holding brass clocks and tasseled lamps. The carpets were so thick I felt unsure of my footing, as if walking in deep grass. Most of Mr. Orlo Pratt's money went into that house and its furnishings, I think. One of the hands told me Madam Blanche had been from the best family in Kansas City, and married Mr. Pratt when he came back there with a railroad car full of horses.

"Up—there?" I asked, incredulous.

Halfway up the stairs toward the rooms where she spent most of her time, she paused, looking back at me.

"Of course," she said, sounding impatient.

Mr. Pratt himself didn't go up those stairs without being invited, and I was scared.

"Well, come on!" She stamped her foot, and I saw an ankle in a flowered slipper—a silken ankle that was at once delicate, and yet somehow strong and full of life.

Swallowing hard, I followed her into the upper hall and toward her bedroom.

Inside she turned, holding out a package.

"Oh, it's so exciting! See what I got for you in Cheyenne City!"

I mumbled something about having to cast up my accounts before suppertime, but she only tossed her head, casually pulling out a comb so that the brassy hair fell in whorls about her cheeks and neck.

"Oh, pshaw, boy! Open the box!"

My fingers groped at the strings. Inside was a leather case, and within that a set of horn-backed combs and brushes, edges glittering dully with what looked like silver. I stared stupidly at them.

"I've been telling Orlo," she said, "that we must do something about that mop of hair, Juanito! If you won't cut it, then we must see it is properly brushed and combed!" Coming close, she took one of the brushes and stroked my hair. I stood like a dumb animal, trembling and scared. In spite of myself, I was excited. My loins tingled with a hot feeling.

"Don't—don't do that!" I muttered.

"Why, what's wrong?" she laughed, coming so close I could smell the Paris scent Mr. Pratt got for her in Cheyenne City. She was a tall woman; with my head bowed for the combing and brushing, my face was only inches from the swell of her breasts, so tightly confined in the velvet bodice they burgeoned like cottonwood buds in the spring. "Juanito, it's only because I like you so! Can't we be friends?"

From below I heard the clatter and jingle of harness, the stamping of hoofs. A cloud of dust rose to Madam Blanche's open window, and I heard rough voices and bantering. Mr. Pratt and the hands were back.

"But where are you going?" Madam Blanche asked. Still holding the brush, she followed me into the hall.

I didn't speak, couldn't speak. Hot and dizzy, ashamed and afraid, I hurried down the stairs and across the pile of the Oriental rugs, her laugh following me. She was still laughing, I think, when Mr. Orlo Pratt went into the house. Later, from my garret room, I heard them arguing. But Madam Blanche's voice was shriller and louder than his. After a while he gave up. A moment later, peeking into the moonlit yard, I saw him stamp into the bunkhouse. I guess that night she didn't want him in the house.

CHAPTER EIGHT

Slash Dollar was a big ranch, bigger than I suspected; even Mr. Pratt didn't know how big it was. On the north his brand went almost to the Laramie River, and on the west to the beginning of the Black Hills. On the east his herds grazed along Cherry Creek and Dry Creek, and on the south his riders rounded up strays in the outskirts of Cheyenne City. He worked hard, I'll say that for him. That summer, especially, there was a lot of rain. A strange disease ran through the herds, so that most of the time he was out with the hands, doctoring sick horses and shooting the sicker ones so they wouldn't infect the rest. He was a rich man, and powerful in that country, but at home Madam Blanche ran the outfit. After that fight they had the night she gave me the brushes, he didn't say much to her any more. But he trusted me more and more with his bills and accounts and land filings and other papers, at the same time leaving me alone with her. *Ohohyaa*—that was very bad! Was he trying to trap me somehow? Neither did I like the way Red and Agustin and the other hands snickered and whispered as I passed the bunkhouse. I did not like the way things were going at all, especially when I remembered the bunkhouse stories about the former bookkeeper, Mr. Boxheimer, who had got too friendly with Mrs. Pratt.

One day, when Mr. Pratt was listening to me read the statement of last month's operations, I made up my mind.

"Sir," I said, "I am tired of keeping these books. I want to go out and help with the horses. After all, I am a good rider and can help a lot in the roundup."

For a moment he did not seem to hear me, only staring out the dirty window and chewing at his mustache.

"Sir," I repeated.

He turned his head, blinking watery eyes. "Eh? What is it, Juan?"

I repeated my request.

"Oh," he said, settling back in his chair and lighting a stogie. "Oh—so you want to help with the horses, eh?"

"Yes, sir," I said.

He took a deep drag on the stogie, puffing out a circle of smoke. "What's the matter with what you're doing? I pay you well. You've got a nice inside job, your own room—" He broke off, staring out the dirty window. "Hell, boy, you got a setup even I can't swing!"

I didn't understand him, and he sensed my bewilderment. He swung to face me, wallowing the stogie around in his mouth. "I be goddam—" he said, then broke off. "You really mean it, boy?"

"Of course I do," I protested. "I've worked cattle and horses before, and I'm a good hand. I don't belong inside here, balancing books and writing letters!"

He looked at me a long time. Then he bit down hard on the cigar and put his boots up on the battered roll-top desk. "No," he said. "Can't be done."

That was all there was to it. He wouldn't say any more. But later I learned Madam Blanche had got wind of my desire to leave the big house, and told her husband she would leave him and go back to Kansas City if he let me ride with the crew. Not only that, but then she made me come to her room every day after supper, to dictate her memoirs.

"You know," she said one day, "I come from a very prominent family in Kansas City. We were all socially minded, we Kittredges."

Lying on the bed in a feathered robe, she smiled at me where I sat on a stool nearby, sheaf of paper in my lap and pen and inkwell to hand. "It seems so long ago now, and so far away," she went on. "Now I live out here in the wilderness, without friends, wasting my life. So—" She patted my hand, and sighed. "You must help me recall those beautiful days in Kansas City, Juanito, so I can have a record of them when I am old and withered and unattractive."

She was all stretched out on the coverlet, small feet pink and bare against the flowered coverlet, and it moved me.

"I can never think of you as old and withered, ma'am," I said.

Instantly, though, I was ashamed of myself. *Sweet Medicine,* I thought, *where are you leading me? This is a white woman, a woman old enough to be my mother!* In panic I fumbled for the *parfleche* cylinder around my neck, then remembered I had hidden it in a bureau drawer lest someone notice it and ask embarrassing questions. I was very glad when she finished her dictation that day and I could get out of her room. *Ohohyaa*! I thought. *What is going on here?*

But I kept on going to her room. She demanded it. And one summer day, the room warm with sun and an occasional honeybee drifting in and out past the lacy curtains, she said something unnerving—to me, at least.

"I know you think me beautiful," she murmured. Her eyes held mine against my will. I tried to turn my head away, but could not. "I can see your love for me," she continued. "You can not hide it, Juanito! Even that first day, when you

came riding across the meadow, I could see it."
Slowly her hand went to her robe. With deliberate
fingers she undid the lacy ties and pulled it aside.
"Do you know what it means to a woman like me
to have someone love her again? Love her, after
so many years?"

The papers fell from my lap, the pen rolled
away, the inkwell dropped on the carpet and
spattered it. Torn between fear and passion, I let
her take my hand and place it on her knee.

"Tell me you love me!" she demanded.

With an effort I managed to draw my hand
away, stooping to pick up the scattered papers.
"Mr. Pratt—" I mumbled. "He—"

"Damn Orlo Pratt!" she cried. She grabbed me,
pulling me down on the bed. "Anyway, he's up
at the Dry Creek line camp, you know that! He
won't be home till Wednesday!" She put one
wrist across her face to shield it from the lamp's
rays, and the long brassy hair fell in waves across
her arm. "Put out the light, Juanito dear. That's a
good boy!"

That night it was raining outside, raining hard;
the drops were loud on the roof in the garret. For
a long time I lay in my narrow bed, looking into
the blackness, hearing the rain, remembering the
scent of her body, the power of her thighs, the
softness of her breasts. Now that I had become a
full man, how far—both in miles and in heart—I
had already strayed from my people!

• • •

I might have stayed on at the Slash Dollar for a long time. After all, I was well paid for what I did, and my duties were casual and slight. I had the run of the house—and nearly every night I went to Madam Blanche's room. In her sumptuous boudoir I learned the secrets of love. She was proud to show me, and I was a willing pupil. Though I did not like to admit it, I was enjoying myself in this white man's world I had conquered so easily. It was heady stuff for an Indian youth who had known only his people's lodges and a miserable boarding school. Shameful to admit, the horse soldier Hazlitt and my vow to the *Tsistsista* faded bit by bit into a secret corner of my brain where I did not often go.

Now Madam seemed to tolerate Mr. Orlo Pratt, even letting him come to her rooms for supper once in a while. She was gay and friendly with him. His eyes lit up when she once in a while patted him on the cheek, calling him "Orlo, dear." To my remembrance, she had never done so before.

Now that the rains had passed, the sun came out every morning hot and burning. The new range grass shriveled and browned in the heat. Madam and I were in her room. It had been torrid that day—the kind of heat that sucks your breath away and makes you restless yet without desire.

"And that," Madam Pratt said, "was when my

157

father bought the street railway company. After that, he—" She broke off and raised herself on an elbow. "Juanito, what's the matter with you? I swear you're not listening."

From somewhere over our heads came a faint rustling noise. I sprang to my feet. I padded to the window. The flowered lace curtains hung listlessly, and in the west there was a faint orange flush where the sun had been.

"I thought I heard something," I whispered.

In silence we both listened. Then Madam Blanche laughed. "Oh, it's just Gerda walking around up in her room!"

I sighed in relief, recognizing the swish of large Scandinavian feet in carpet slippers.

"Wait a minute," she urged. "Stay there for a minute!" Staring at me, Madam crossed her arms behind her head and lay propped on the pillows. "My dear, I love to look at you like that! So tall, so slender, so—so *boyish,* in a way, and yet so—well, *virile* is all I can say! Ah, these days I'm happy for the first time since I came to this desolate place! Can you understand that, Juanito?"

Almost wearily I lay back down beside her, picking up my notebook.

"Yes, ma'am," I said. "Now your father had just bought the street railway company."

She looked at me strangely.

"Yes," she murmured. "Yes, that's right."

After that there was a coolness between us for a day or so, but it soon disappeared in the heat of her passion. We stayed long hours in the brass bed, even until the frost came and the leaves on the trees turned red and then brown and began to fall.

It rained again in October. The downpour stripped the last leaves from the trees, and they stood gaunt and dismal in the yard. Winds howled round the gables of the big house, and I huddled in the tiny office-shed, adding columns of figures. When the soldiers rode up Mr. Pratt and some of the hands, wearing yellow slickers, were out in the rain fixing fence posts that had rotted off at ground level.

Startled, I rubbed my hand against the dirty window to get a better view. They were cavalrymen; I recognized the sodden cavalry greatcoats with the yellow piping. One of them, I thought, looked like Sergeant Garrity. What were they doing here?

My heart in my throat, I let myself silently out of the door. Keeping the shed between the riders and me, I ran across the wet grass, sliding and sloshing, into the house. Gerda, endlessly dusting furniture, looked at me, then went on about her work. I ran to Madam's room and knocked.

"Come in!" she called. "Is that you, Juanito?"

I hurried in, closing the door after me, and went to the window that overlooked the yard.

Wide-eyed, she sat in the middle of the bed, holding the coverlet about her breasts. "Whatever is the matter?"

"Nothing," I said.

That *was* Garrity, I was sure of it. I could almost hear his Irish brogue as he talked to Mr. Orlo Pratt.

"Stay there!" I said sharply when she tried to rise, one hand reaching for her gown.

Slowly her hand drew back, her face incredulous. "Why, Juanito, are you giving *me* orders now?"

Standing at the edge of the window, hidden by the curtains, I watched the soldiers. Garrity—at least I thought it was Garrity—followed Mr. Pratt to the office-shed. They went inside while the mounted troopers fidgeted dismally in the rain. One of them lit a pipe and held his oilcloth cap over it. Another took a lump of hardtack out of his pocket and gnawed on it.

"Will you explain to me—" Madam began crossly.

"Not now," I pleaded. "Later!"

What were they doing in that shed? Through the rain-streaked window I could see them move dimly about in the office. Any moment I expected Mr. Pratt to come out of the door and call for me, or worse, to come into the house and get me.

After what seemed an hour, the noncom in his mud-caked boots tramped out, and he and Mr.

160

Pratt shook hands. A moment later the little band rode away, easterly, toward Fort McPherson. I never found out if it was Garrity. I never even found out what they wanted. Perhaps it was only to arrange the purchase of some horses, or hay, or feed, or something else. Mr. Pratt never said, and I was afraid to ask. Maybe they had even asked him if he had seen a Cheyenne boy wanted for murder, and maybe he had said no. He would have done that, I think, if he had suspected I was that boy. But it was still a frightening experience, making me realize in what danger I still was. So one day, one of the rare days he was at the house, I told Mr. Pratt what I planned to do.

"Eh?" He looked startled.

"Yes, sir," I repeated. "I want to go with that shipment of horses to Salt Lake City. I—I— well, I've always heard about the Mormons and their curious ways, and I want to see the sights of the town and the Great Salt Lake." Though I didn't tell him, of course, the faded clipping my grandfather showed me so long ago said Hazlitt had gone to Fort Douglas, near Salt Lake City, to take over the headquarters of the 6th Cavalry.

He got out a plug of cable twist, sawing off a piece with his penknife. "I got a full crew all laid out for Salt Lake City."

"You can put me in place of Agustin or Red

161

Gulick or any of the hands," I insisted. "I'm a good man with horses, and I've never had a chance to show it around here." When he hesitated, I went on. "I guess it's only fair to tell you I'm not coming back, either."

It seemed to hit him like a thunderbolt. He sat down in the chair, putting the bit of plug into his mouth as if he weren't paying any attention to what it was. After a while his jaws started to work, almost like a jointed toy of some sort. "You're not coming back?" he asked.

"No."

His voice was almost inaudible. "Mind telling me why?"

A mature man would have been more cautious, but I just blurted it out.

"Because," I said, "I hate myself and what I'm doing here. I never wanted to hurt you, Mr. Pratt. I—I never wanted to do anything, but work and get ahead. But I—well, I got into something and I'm sorry and now I'm going away."

His face worked, and he chewed at his mustache.

"Don't worry about anything," I said. "My mind's made up. I'll tell her, if you don't want to."

He sat there a long time, chewing, looking at his boots propped on the desk, seeming to listen to the rain. Once he reached out and flicked a chunk of mud from the heel of his boot. When it fell to the floor he looked carefully at it, cocking his head this way and that as if it were something new and strange.

"Well?" I said.

Mr. Pratt got to his feet. He went to the big iron safe and squatted in front of it. This way so many times, that way, back again. Twisting the brass lever, he pulled the door open and took out a sheaf of greenbacks. Carefully he wet his thumb and counted out a thick stack. Then, after deliberating a moment, he added a few more.

"Here," he said, getting up and handing the wad to me. "Take this, boy."

I drew back. "I don't need any money, sir. I've been saving my wages, and—"

"Take it!" Angrily he thrust it at me. I was amazed to see he was crying. Tears welled into his eyes, ran down the furrows in his cheeks, leaked into the stained mustache. "Goddam it, boy, take it! Don't make me stand here and beg you!"

I didn't know what to say. Why did Mr. Orlo Pratt insist on giving me money, a lot of money? I guess my face betrayed my puzzlement.

"Look here," Mr. Pratt said, more calmly, but still trying to put the money into my hand. "It's hard to understand, I guess, especially for a boy like you. But I gave her everything, understand? Nothing was ever too good for her, or will be! I never spared any expense. But some things you can't buy for money, see? And that's what she wanted. That's what she *had* to have, and I couldn't give it to her no more. So you made her happy. I love her, no matter what she thinks of me. It's been a privilege for a used-up old man like me, and I'm grateful for it. So take this and—"

Embarrassed, bewildered, near tears myself, I pushed away the money and hurried back into the house, leaving him standing there with the bills. I told Madam Blanche what I was going to do. She was incredulous.

"You'll never go!" Firmly she shook her head. She had heated a curling iron over a small alcohol burner and was doing her hair. I remember the room was full of the smell of burning hair.

"You'll never go!" she repeated. "You love me, Juanito! And that's why you won't go."

It was no use to argue. But one rainy morning I left with the last drive to the railhead at Cheyenne City. Mr. Pratt made room for me on the crew and I moved out after the hands had gone, driving the chuckwagon.

Nobody said goodbye. Mr. Pratt stayed in the office, busy over the books he was going to have to keep himself. After what happened between us, I guess he didn't want to talk to me any more. Maybe he was embarrassed about crying. I was sad he felt that way, because he was always good to me and I liked him. But when I found myself thinking that way, it made me suddenly angry. Why should I feel sorry for *any* white man? All they ever did was cheat us and drive us from our hunting grounds and spill our blood. The very land Slash Dollar occupied used to belong to us! Passion rose in me, and I stood up in the wagon and slashed the reins across the backs of the mules. They broke into a gallop, and I had to calm them down and coax them back to their usual shamble.

At the turn of the road, down by the end of the lane of cottonwood trees, I turned to look at the big house. Maybe the curtains at the upstairs window moved a little; I don't know. It was too far to tell.

I had never seen anything like the place where the Mormons lived. Even my recollection of Grandfather's village, in its great days when there were over a thousand warriors and three thousand ponies, did not begin to approach the size of Salt Lake City. Lying to the east of the Great Lake, a huge and strange spectacle in its own right, the Mormons under Mr. Young had laid out an immense village, regular and right-angled as the spaces of a checkerboard.

On the cars we had spent three days with the shipment of horses. I never wanted to see that country again. It was dry and dead-looking for the most part, an earth with all the juice sucked from it. Westward the locomotive chuffed its way, dragging and jerking our cars—Laramie, Cooper Lake, Separation, Green River, Rock Springs, Hanging Rock, Devil's Gate. Then a new engine switched us to the branch line, and it was jerk, bang, crash all over again; Kaysville, Farmington, Center City, and finally the city of the Mormons.

Salt Lake City gladdened my heart, especially the trees. They were not, of course, like the trees around Grandfather's Village, or the few that soldiers had planted on the barren plains of Fort McPherson. These were what a man told me were Lombardy poplars; tall delicate trees with thread-suspended leaves that trembled in the slightest breeze.

The Mormons were busy people. Everywhere they rushed about, in gray homespun and floppy felt hats and heavy cowhide shoes, going about their business with speed and purpose that kept me goggle-eyed. They raised huge amounts of peaches, grapes, currants, wheat, oats, corn, and other things I didn't recognize. Mormon carts and wagons choked the dusty streets as people labored like ants to store away produce for the winter. But unlike ants (so far as I know anything about ants) the Mormons were religious, pausing in the middle of a busy street to take off their hats and say a prayer to their *Heammawihio*, whoever he was. On every corner was a Ward

House where they went to worship at nights and twice on Sunday, and at dawn every morning a man came out in the public square and played a selection on the bugle—an old Mormon hymn. I learned the words, but that is another story. They went like this:

"O ye mountains high,
O Zion dear Zion, land of the free!
Now my own mountain home,
To thee I have come."

I can't say the tune appealed to me, especially when I wanted to sleep in the morning. Even when the snows were heavy on the Wasatch Mountains, coming right down into the city to lie two or three inches deep over the box-like houses, that man would come out and blow his bugle and everybody would rush out and start to work again.

At the Slash Dollar I had saved almost fifty dollars. Since it was all I had in the world I didn't want to spend it, so I spent the nights huddled in an old Slash Dollar blanket around a fire by the UP tracks with a lot of strange people. Some were miners with no claims, others down-at-the-heel railroad men or just plain vagabonds, with a sprinkling of mountain men and drovers. They had a small camp along the tracks, and carried on a running war with the Mormons. My camp companions were all Gentiles, they said, which I didn't understand but figured it meant not Mormon, anyway.

"They don't cotton to anyone ain't a relative of Brigham Young," a grizzled old brakeman wearing a topless plug hat told me, "and that takes in a lot of territory." He stirred the stew we all shared in. "Now look at me, a good Baptist, been accepted everyplace including Denver! But when I put a foot in this damned town, they act like I smelled bad!"

He did, too, but I saw his point.

"As for Mexicans and Injuns," the brakeman went on, "a Mormon don't consider them human. Greasers and Injuns—anyone with a dark face— is left over from the Lost Tribes of Israel, and a good Mormon spits on 'em!"

I had already felt this in my walks through the city, and changed my identity again. Fortunately, the French name for a beaver is the same as in Spanish—*castor.* But I had to change my first name a little. Now I was Jean Castor, son of French parents who lived in—where? I furrowed my brow, trying to remember my geography book at the Indian Salvation School. Mont Saint Michel? No, that was in France. Montgomery? Well, Mont something. Montreal, that was it!

"I'm a Canadian," I volunteered, holding out my tin cup for a dipper of the communal stew. "How would they feel about a Canadian?"

168

He looked at me, pursing his lips in the thicket of beard.

"Never heered," he said. "Maybe that'd do the trick." Sticking a dirty thumb at my chest, he wanted to know what that thing was around my neck.

"Oh," I said, tucking the *parfleche* cylinder out of sight, "just a—well, a kind of a charm."

"You're Catholic, eh?"

"Yes," I lied, hoping the falsehood would satisfy him. But then he went off on a scurrilous attack of the Pope, so when I had a chance I moved away and sat down to finish my stew in the jumble of old ties where I slept at night.

Next day I went into the city to see what I could find out about the horse soldier Hazlitt. The tattered clipping my grandfather showed me said Hazlitt had gone to Fort Douglas. But that had been a long time ago. Where was he now? Trying out my new identity as a French Canadian (after all, that was what my other grandfather was) I stopped in the offices of the *Deseret News*.

"I dunno," a surly man in eyeshade and elegant sleeve guards said. It was evident he took me for a Gentile. I almost laughed out loud, thinking what his ugly face would look like if he knew what I really was—a Cheyenne warrior, on the trail of the scalp of a late citizen of their area. "I dunno," he repeated. "Was transferred to Californy somewhere, as I recollect. Heard he was a general now. Sacramento, maybe it was."

When I pressed him to look through his back files for more information, he got very angry and swore. Mormon swearing is a peculiar thing. When they are indignant, they all (including some of the women) say, "I'll be go to hell!" It is not grammatical, but seems a favorite oath. And when they are disgusted, or don't believe something, they all cry "Bear's ass!" I don't know what the back end of a bear has to do with anything, but that's what they say in moments of stress. The unpleasant man in the sleeve guards used both of these expressions, and some more. "I got a paper to print!" he finished. "Now go away and leave me in peace, will you?"

He was so mad he didn't notice me pick up the latest issue of the *News* from the table and put it under my coat. Later, I sat under a poplar tree in the winter sun, reading it from front page to back, hoping for information that might lead me to the horse soldier Hazlitt. Suddenly I sat upright, my heart racing. On an inside page, near the bottom, was a brief news item headed INDIAN UNREST:

Reports from Fort McPherson, Nebraska, say that the Cheyenne Indians, recently removed from their villages and resettled at the fort, are approaching a state of insurrection. The Army reports that several ringleaders, among them savages

with the interesting names of Gentle
Horse and Strong Left Hand, have been
jailed in an effort to end the unrest.

My grandfather! And his friend who found me
in the snowstorm, that time so long ago when I
fled the school, and saved my life! Dumbly I sat
there, not seeing the newspaper clutched in my
hands. So that was what those new wooden sheds
were at Fort McPherson, the ones they were
building along the river at the time I ran away!
They were sheds for my people, the *Tsistsista*!
Cattle barns, that was what they were; cattle
barns for people treated like cattle, driven off
their lands and imprisoned at Fort McPherson!

Throwing down the paper, I rushed through the
square. In my impatience I shouldered people
aside and knocked over a handbarrow filled with
cabbages. The man swore after me, shaking a
Mormon fist, but I didn't pay any attention.

At the railroad tracks I knelt and reached back
into the pile of ties, searching for my blanket
and other things I kept there. The rest of the
"Gentiles" watched me.

"What's the matter, sonny?" a lounging miner
asked.

Fifty dollars was enough to pay my fare to
Sacramento and then some. What was I doing
here in Salt Lake City, wasting time, while my
grandfather languished in jail? What had I been

doing on the Slash Dollar ranch, lolling pampered in Madam Blanche's bed, while the *Tsistsista* were hounded to jail at Fort McPherson? My cheeks burned in shame.

"Something wrong?" a man in dirty buckskins asked.

Incredulously I stared at the blanket, laid flat on the dirt. My money was gone! I snatched at the blanket, turned it over, shook it out, stared at it again.

"My money!" I cried. "It's been stolen!"

The miner and the trapper and a few others formed a ring around me. The man tending the stew sauntered up, licking a greasy spoon, and asked, "Money? Who around here had money to be stole?"

The miner took my arm in his brawny fist, and asked very quietly, "You had money rolled in that blanket?"

"Of course!" I blurted. "I had nearly fifty dollars hid in there!"

The miner took a long knife from his belt and picked his thumbnail with it. Things were suddenly very quiet. The miner seemed angry; why, I didn't know. He shook me, saying, "Come off it, boy! There ain't that much money in the world!"

It must have seemed like a lot to them, too. They were all down-at-the-heel and might have starved if it wasn't for the stewpot filled with spoiled vegetables and scraps of meat they managed to steal.

"I swear it!" I cried. "My pay from the Slash Dollar Ranch!" I looked desperately around, searching for a remembered face. "Where's that man in the broken plug hat—the brakeman? He took my money!"

There was silence. Then a man said, "If it's the galoot with the busted hat, he got on the train for Ogden City this morning. Said he had relations in Omaha he hadn't seen for a spell."

The miner was still holding my arm. Some of the others moved close around me, looking ugly. What was the matter with them? I was the injured party, wasn't I? Suddenly I winced as the miner's powerful fingers dug into my arm.

"You mean to tell me, sonny, you had fifty dollars in your poke and didn't share none of it with us?"

Startled, I blinked at him. "Why, no," I said. "I guess I didn't think—that is, I mean I—"

As he twisted my arm behind me, I almost let out a cry of pain.

"Why, you goddam little sneak!" the man with the cook spoon yelled. Grabbing a handful of my shirt front, he twisted it till buttons popped off. "If you had all that money, what in hell was you doing eating us poor men's grub and sponging off'n us?"

"Yeah!" someone else shouted. "Why in hell wasn't you living in style down at the Drover's Hotel 'stead of mooching off honest men?"

With an oath the miner hurled me from him. I went sprawling backward among my few possessions.

"We share and share alike here!" he growled. "Ain't no room for them that holds out on their mates!"

The trapper let fly with the knife. I don't think he actually meant to hit me, but the blade hissed through the air and stood quivering in the earth a finger's thickness from my ear. *Ohohyaa.* Very bad.

"Git out!" someone yelled, and threw a fist-sized stone.

"And don't come back!" another man called, looking round for more rocks to fling.

If I'd had time, I would have liked to explain I was saving my money for a great purpose, and couldn't share it with them, much as I'd have liked to. After all, it was only fair. But there wasn't time for anything but to snatch up my blanket, dump the comb and tincup and spoon and matches into it, and throw it over my shoulder like a knapsack. After that I ran, and ran, and ran; a long way I ran, paralleling the UP tracks toward town.

Finally, beyond pursuit, I sat down on a grassy hillock and rested, my sides heaving like bellows.

Grandfather, I said to myself, *it will take a little longer than I thought. But do not worry. I am still ho nuh ka wa, the Bearer of the Thunder Bow, and I will do what I have sworn to do.*

CHAPTER NINE

On the Slash Dollar I had done despicable things, things that made me ashamed when I thought about them. Yet I pleased Madam Blanche, and her husband tried to give me money when I left. On the other hand I never did anything wrong in the City of the Mormons, except maybe lie a little, but they took offense and drove me from Salt Lake City. There is no understanding the reasoning of white people.

Discouraged, penniless, and alone, I finally drifted back to the square and sat there, chin on my chest. It was late afternoon and the sun was going down. Already the air was chill and sharp. When I had sat here a few hours before, I was a rich man, nearly fifty dollars rich. Then I could afford to be tolerant, amused by the queer people who thronged the square. I had even laughed at the angry man in the office of the *Deseret News*, considering myself vastly superior to him. Now the tables were turned. Sacramento was hundreds of miles away. In thin shirt and pants I shivered on a park bench in a strange land, no way to survive except to depend on the charity of white people, Mormons at that!

Miserable, I drew my feet under me and squatted on the bench with the blanket wrapped around my shoulders. The few late passersby didn't pay any attention to me. Lights—warm yellow lights—winked on in the windows of the boxy houses. In the distance the snowy Wasatch was tipped with pink as the last rays of the sun touched the peaks. There is a time, at the precise moments of sunrise and sunset, when the gods pause in their work and listen especially hard to the pleas of the *Tsistsista. Sweet Medicine,* I prayed, holding the leather cylinder in my hands, *look down on your poor child and tell him what to do. He has work to do, great work, the cleansing of our Sacred Arrows. Yet some kind of a mohin must be on his back, pulling him down and sucking the strength from his body and the brains from his head.*

I think in my grief and desolation I even gave an animal-like howl. A stout man leading a mule paused and looked at me.

"Are you in pain, sonny?" he asked.

Not knowing what to say, I shook my head and he moved on in the gathering dusk. After that, afraid I would be overheard and put in jail as a menace to society (the Mormons must have had a jail, though I never saw one) I limited myself to gesturing in sign language, knowing *Sweet Medicine* could see me and understand even in the dark.

I am the weapon of my people, I signed. *I am Bearer of the Thunder Bow, though you would not think it to see me now. It is up to me to find the horse soldier Hazlitt, and wipe away the bloodstains so that the Tsistsista will again become great and powerful, and so return to the lands whence they were driven.*

At first I didn't notice, but soon became aware of a black-bearded man in a long frock coat standing near me, a book tucked under his arm, peering through gold-rimmed spectacles.

"I be go to hell!" he cried.

I didn't know what to say. Things couldn't be any worse. But maybe the jail was warm anyway.

"I was just saying my prayers," I told him.

"You ain't one of us," he said, looking puzzled.

"That's right," I agreed.

"You look like an Injun," he pointed out, "sitting there all swaddled up in a blanket."

Whatever I admitted, I figured I had better not claim to be an Indian in Salt Lake City. There were a few so-called Indians around the square—beggars mostly—called Paiutes. They were the sorriest-looking things I had seen in a long time.

"No," I explained, "though I've traveled a lot in Sioux and Cheyenne country as a trapper, and know their ways. Actually, I was born in

Montreal of French parents, but sometimes I pray in the Indian sign language. Saves my voice when I've got a bad cold, like now. Actually, I'm a Catholic."

It was the damnedest lie anyone ever told. My voice did indeed almost fail when I told it.

"Catholic," he muttered, saying the word like I'd just told him I was a rattlesnake. "Ummm— well!" He took the book from under his arm. "An interesting way to talk to your god, or whatever Catholics call him." He held out the book, pointing at a line. "Can you read?"

"Of course," I said.

"Then read me this." When I began, pulling the book close to my nose in the failing light, he interrupted me. "I don't mean *read*—I mean to put what you see in the Book of Mormon into those gestures you were making!"

It wasn't hard; after all, back at the Indian Salvation School I used to amuse Cora Parsley by putting Shakespeare's *Sonnets* into hand language.

> And when he had spoken unto them, he turned himself unto the three and said unto them, What will ye that I should do unto you when I am gone unto the Father? And they sorrowed in their hearts, for they durst not speak unto him the thing which they desired.

There was a lot more of it, all about three old men called the Nephites, whom I gathered were some kind of angels for the Mormons. Finally I couldn't read any more in the dark, and I gave up. The bearded man took the book from me, and stood for a moment polishing his glasses with a handkerchief.

"Remarkable," he said. "Very beautiful the way you do that, Mr.—Mr.—"

"Castor," I said. "Jean Castor, sir. It's the French word for 'beaver.' "

He looked me up and down, still polishing his spectacles.

"I take it you are without a situation?"

It was a new word to me, and I looked puzzled.

"I mean, you don't have a job right now."

"That's right," I said. "As a matter of fact, I've fallen on evil times. A rascal stole my money. I had been intending to visit California, but now I am penniless."

He huffed on the spectacles, and put them back on his nose.

"Well," he said, "I've got something in mind, Mr. Castor. If you care to come along with me, I'll see that you have a bed for the night, and food. Tomorrow we'll talk about my idea."

"That's very kind of you," I said, falling into step with him but walking a little behind. I knew my place, and didn't want to press my luck. Suddenly he turned round, staring at me over the gold rims. "My name's Isaac Barley," he said, and went on trudging down the line of oil lamps a man on a stepladder was lighting. I followed him, still walking a little behind. I didn't know what was going to happen, but *Sweet Medicine* did; once again he had showed me the way.

It was ironic; the farthest thing from my mind was to become a missionary to any Indians, especially to those woebegone Paiutes I saw in the public square. But that seemed to be the way *Sweet Medicine* had me pointed, at least for the moment. So I went along.

Isaac Barley turned out to be a prominent Mormon, a mainstay of the church and a kind and respected man. He lived in a big brick house at the edge of town with two wives. Abigail, the first and principal one, who ran the household, was a tall rawboned woman with a big nose and a shiny face, graying hair pulled back with a brooch. Rebecca was small and frail, much younger, with pale blue eyes and hair so fine and fair it looked like white silk. When we got there, Mr. Barley called them both in, eager and enthusiastic, and said, "Ladies, I want you to see this!"

He had them sit down while I went through my sign language demonstration of the passage from the Book of Mormon.

"There!" he cried when I was done. "Ain't that remarkable, ladies?"

Rebecca laughed and clapped her hands. "Marvelous!" she cried. "So beautiful, so graceful! I admire it, husband, and—"

"I don't see," Abigail interrupted, "what possible use it is. Pretty, maybe, but—"

"Mr. Castor," Isaac Barley said, "for that is his name, is of French descent. He's traveled a lot among the Indian tribes. Jasper Pope and I were talking the other day—you remember I mentioned it, Abigail—how we've got to reach these poor benighted Paiute savages of ours. What better way than a man who knows Indians, speaks their jabber, can talk to them and bring the Lord's word to savage hearts?"

The two wives were surprised, but I was stunned.

"Fifty a month, and found," Mr. Barley proposed. "Will you take the job, Mr. Castor?"

The upshot of it was that I agreed to try it out for a while, and that night I slept warm and comfortable in a bed with a feather mattress and comforter.

Early next morning Mr. Barley came into my room. I didn't wake till he threw up the shades. The clatter roused me. Still half asleep, wariness governed my actions. I rolled out of bed and dropped behind it, frightened. When I peered out, Mr. Barley was standing there in his underclothes,

181

laughing. "Scared you, did I?" he asked. "Well, Mr. Castor, it's time to rise and shine. There's a lot to do today."

I never saw such fancy underwear—so white and fine it glittered like snow in the winter sun streaming through the windows. Later I found that was the custom of the Mormons. No matter what their outward dress, underneath they wore consecrated garments kept clean and pressed so they were like new. It was an article of their faith.

Mr. Barley took me on a walking tour of the city, and it was easy to see from the way people greeted him, all smiles and politeness, that he was an important man. Though I wasn't allowed in, not being one of the faithful, he showed me the outside of the Great Tabernacle. "Two hundred and fifty feet by a hundred and fifty," he said, "and seventy feet high. Holds ten thousand people, Mr. Castor."

We also ran into a Mr. John Thomas, who was president of the Church, whatever that meant. My benefactor introduced me and told Mr. Thomas about his plans for me, which the president liked and said so.

"Fine man," Mr. Barley said, watching Mr. Thomas go into the Temple. "A great worker and a dedicated man."

Dedicated man? That made me start a little. But Mr. Barley had me by the arm, pulling me down the street. "Now we'll drop in on Jasper Pope," he said.

On the way I was taken by the painted and engraved and printed honeybees I saw on shop-windows, storefronts, bookcovers, everywhere.

"Mr. Castor," Isaac Barley explained, "that's the symbol—the real symbol—of the Mormon faith. *Deseret*, the word itself—it means 'honey-bee.' We labor like honeybees, all of us in this promised land, for the greater glory of the Lord."

I had thought the Mormons acted more like ants, but if it was honeybees they were, it was all right with me.

When he took me to the offices of the *Deseret News*, I pulled back, remembering my meeting with the clerk the day before. But it turned out worse than I feared. The red-faced man in the elegant sleeve garters was Jasper Pope, editor of the paper. He remembered me.

"We've met," he told Mr. Barley, but didn't say anything more, just kept watching me like I had the smallpox.

"Oh!" said Mr. Barley in some surprise. "Well, that's nice! For this young man may have the key to a business that's plagued the Church for a long time, Jasper."

He went on to tell the editor about his plans for my missionary work. I don't think Jasper Pope liked the idea too well, but when Mr. Barley explained that John Thomas approved the proposition, Mr. Pope didn't say much more, though he continued to look sour.

That night they rousted up a bunch of the Paiutes and sat them down on folding chairs in a big room of a Ward House. There seemed to be a Ward House on every street. Later I found the whole city was divided up into wards. The Ward House was a place where the neighborhood people could come each day to pray or do good works or have church dinners or maybe just sit and knit socks for the heathen Paiutes.

A lot of Mormons were at the Ward House that night. Most of the men and women dressed very plain. Abigail and Rebecca attended, and even Mr. Thomas, the president of the Church. Jasper Pope was there, too, very elegant for a Mormon in a flowered vest with a big gold watch chain across it, and carrying a gold-headed cane. He seemed to have special status, bowed and scraped to more than reasonable for a newspaper editor, and took charge of the events, leading the congregation in a long and windy hymn entitled "Do What Is Right, Let the Consequences Follow."

The frightened Paiutes sat huddled on folding chairs, looking about with eyes that sometimes rolled up to show the whites. They were skinny and knobby-kneed, most of them; even though this was a winter night, with snow on the Wasatch and an iron stove glowing red near the stage, the poor fellows wore only the scantiest of cast-off white man's clothing, threadbare at that, with verminous blankets wrapped round some.

Finally my turn came. Mr. Barley introduced me, giving a brief talk on the plight of the Paiutes, and how he proposed to hire me as a missionary to bring them the word of God.

"Now," Mr. Barley said, "I'm going to call on our friend Mr. Castor to interpret for me. I want to address these poor dumb brutes, tell them how we love them and have their best interests at heart, how they must receive the message of the Lord and become docile and hard-working like the rest of us in this land of milk and honey."

With a nod to me, he started on a long speech. I stood beside him, putting the words into the hand language that all the Cheyenne and Sioux and Crow and Blackfoot and Arapaho understood. Would these poor Paiutes understand? Anxiously I looked for comprehension, even interest.

"—Lost Tribes of Israel," Mr. Barley was saying. "For that is what you truly are, and being lost, you've got to be found. Ain't that reasonable?"

Still I searched for a glimmer of understanding. But at last, figuring I had made a fool of Mr. Barley and myself into the bargain, I saw one leathery face break into a smile. The man, a skinny rack of bones wearing a motheaten saddle blanket and little else, nodded, saying something to a vacant-faced man next to him. Then they both nodded, bobbing their heads like mechanical toys.

"We are getting through to them," Mr. Barley muttered to me, and went on with his speech.

After a while my feet began to hurt from standing so long. The Mormons seemed entranced, watching my gestures with open mouths and an occasional expression of approval, but the whole thing was getting boring to me. The Paiutes were bored, too; they didn't take much stock in anything a white man told them. So to refresh their interest, I experimented with Mr. Barley's words. When he spoke of the land of milk and honey, I pointed out to the Paiutes that the land really belonged to them. When he bragged about how prosperous Salt Lake City was, I called the attention of the Paiutes to their own skinny ribs and shabby garments. When he mentioned the word of the Lord, I made it clear it was the white man's Lord he referred to, and that the Paiutes had their own *Heammawihio* who was just as powerful. As Mr. Barley ended an hour and a half of oratory, I threw in a few sign-language thoughts of my own, to the effect that maybe the Paiutes ought to give Mr. Barley's proposition a try, but there was always the possibility of throwing the rascals clear out of Paiute lands and taking over some milk and honey for themselves.

Even being modest about it, that night I was a

sensation. The Paiutes surrounded the dais and threw their arms about me, calling me "brother," and promising to go wherever I should lead them. The Mormons, of course, didn't understand a word of the palaver except that I seemed to have a powerful effect on the Paiutes. Mr. Barley looked dazed, passing a hand over his brow and dabbing at sweat with a pocket handkerchief. "I'll be go to hell!" he kept saying. "Imagine it! The power of the Lord!"

Abigail shook my hand limply but Rebecca squeezed my arm hard, blue eyes dancing. "Mr. Castor!" she cried, "it was so—so *poetic!* Like music, almost, the way you did it! And we know that music hath charms to soothe the savage breast!"

Only Mr. Jasper Pope seemed reserved. He stood near me until Rebecca, feeling him close by, grew uncomfortable and withdrew, after making me promise to speak at her ladies' group on "The Red Indians and Their Curious Customs." Mr. Pope, picking his teeth with a gold toothpick, watched her go, then turned to me.

"You seemed," he said, "to have a remarkable hold on these poor heathen, Mr. Castor. Why, they listened to your every word—or I guess a better way of saying it is your every gesture—like starving people who have been promised food! None of us ever managed to come so close to them."

"Thank you very much," I said.

"Some day soon," he went on, "you must come to the offices of the *News* and tell me about yourself and your experiences. A long feature article would be well received by our readers."

As he left, still chewing on his toothpick, he swung sharply round. "*Au revoir*," he barked.

I didn't know much French, but I knew enough to wish him goodbye.

"*A bientôt*," I called, and watched him disappear in the crowd.

In spite of myself, I came to be interested in those poor Paiutes. They were a bedraggled and spineless lot, but some of them tried hard, and others showed more sense than I hoped. Mr. Barley found I knew something about horses and cows and farming and that got him started on plans for a kind of farm-asylum where the Paiutes could learn agricultural skills and maybe grammar and arithmetic, too. Rebecca was interested, too, and in her sweet way tried to help me.

"For," she said, "they are God's children, too, are they not, though of a lower order than we are?"

I felt sorry for Rebecca. The Mormon system was authoritarian, fine for the men but to my mind keeping the women almost as slaves, to cook and scrub and mend clothes and bear children. I could see their hunger for freedom in the way Rebecca wanted to talk to me all the time, in the way she begged me to tell her of books to read so that she might improve her conversation, the way the ladies of her club hung on my every word when I talked to them, as I did frequently. A senior wife like Abigail, who was a strong woman anyhow, got along pretty well, but poor Rebecca was only a child, and a neglected one at that, hungry for love and understanding and respect.

"Well," I said, "some people are of a lower order than others, that's true." It was all I could say without betraying myself.

I gave regular religious lectures to the Paiutes that spring, getting to know some of them quite well, and to like one in particular. Sanitary Sam was the skinny man who had first seemed to understand me that night at the Ward House. Big-nosed and flat-footed, he was the butt of constant jokes by the Mormons he came into contact with. Sam came by his name because, somehow or other, the Mormons had gotten through to him, even if nothing else registered, that cleanliness was next to godliness. He was always dousing himself in a horse trough, scraping his ancient skin with a handful of dry corn shucks, begging soap from anyone who would listen.

In a way, I was happy in the City of the Mormons. Mr. Barley was kind to me, giving me a gold watch inscribed with his name and thanks for being such a help in his good works to the Paiutes. Though not a Mormon, I was known and respected in the community, even convincing myself I was bettering the plight of my Paiute brothers. I did not quite understand what *Sweet Medicine* had in mind for me, but each night before I slept I put the *parfleche* cylinder around my neck and prayed for a sign. None came, but I slept comfortably. It was better than the Gentiles' camp along the railroad tracks, and if it had not been for that damned bugler waking me early every morning, life would have been ideal.

Mr. Jasper Pope continued to worry me, however. Frequently he came to the Ward House where I was instructing my Paiute charges, watching hour after hour, saying nothing and toying with the gold watch chain. He never spoke further about an article for the *Deseret News*, only watched, and perhaps waited; for what I did not know. But a confrontation was coming, I felt it in my bones. One day it did come, with a suddenness and violence that startled me.

It happened this way. I was sitting in the Ward House, leafing through some books on husbandry Mr. Barley had bought me, while my Paiutes frolicked outside in the sunshine, waiting for me to summon them for instruction. Of late they had developed a little spirit, and now joked among themselves and showed a developing personal pride in themselves and their tribe.

I heard a scuffling sound outside, and sharp cries. Hurrying out, I found that Sanitary Sam, bathing from a battered bucket, had overturned it and soaked Mr. Jasper Pope's boots and trouser legs with dirty water. Mr. Pope, on hand for his regular inspection of my classes, was furious.

"Take that!" he shouted, knocking Sam sprawling with a blow of his cane. "Damned savage! What in hell do you think you're doing, washing your mangy hide on a public side-walk?"

Immediately the rest of the Paiutes swarmed about Mr. Pope, snarling at him like a pack of dogs and knocking his hat off. It startled him, never having seen these poor people show any emotion but servility.

"Sam!" I called. "Drop that rock!" I pushed the others away, standing between them and Mr. Pope. "I'm sorry," I explained, "but you shouldn't have caned old Sam, Mr. Pope. He didn't mean any harm."

"Bear's ass!" Mr. Pope snapped. He picked up his hat and jammed it on his head. Sam, contrite, tried to brush off his sleeve, but Mr. Pope shoved him away.

"I hold you responsible for this, Mr. Castor!" he cried. "We never had any trouble with the Indians till you came around here, sir! Why, from the way you take up for them, I'd suspect you were an Indian yourself!"

I caught my breath at that, but didn't say anything.

"Sometimes I think," he went on, becoming a little calmer and therefore more dangerous, "that we don't know nearly enough about you, Mr. Castor, to trust you with such a large undertaking. Oh, I know you've taken in old Isaac Barley and his friends, but *I'm* not sure." Idly he reached forward, touching the *parfleche* cylinder that hung round my neck. In the scuffle it had popped out of my shirt and lay on my chest.

"What is this?" he asked.

I swallowed hard. "Nothing. Just a—well, a kind of a medallion, you could call it."

He looked me in the eye, smiling a little, fingers again working at his gold watch chain. "You're Catholic, Isaac Barley tells me."

"Yes," I said.

With one finger he flicked *Sweet Medicine*, making it swing back and forth on my chest.

"It looks Indian to me," he said. "Like something a Sioux or Cheyenne might wear. I've seen them before." When I started to stammer something he turned away, swinging his cane, spruce and dapper, and walked rapidly toward the *Deseret News* office.

I told Mr. Barley what had happened and he was indignant. "He shouldn't have beaten the man," he said. "I'll have to have a talk with him. But you must understand, Mr. Castor, that Jasper

Pope is a godly man. Perhaps he was brushed against by the Devil for a moment, but this will pass. And you ain't to worry about your status here. Jasper is powerful in our councils, but I have friends too."

That night I lay fully dressed for a long time in my room, reading. It was spring, and the room was filled with cool night and lantern-shine. The rays of the Argand lamp lit the pages of Meacham's *Agricultural Mechanics and the Principles of Husbandry*, but my mind wasn't on the book. I let it fall shut on my chest, and stared into the hot core of the lamp wick. After a while it seemed to have a hypnotic effect, and I felt almost as if my soul and body had separated. My body still lay on the bed while my spirit hovered in the air, floating about the room, asking questions. In a way, it was like a dream. But not exactly; I really hadn't had any good dreams for a long time now. It was more like some strange person was trying to talk to me, to make me see things his way.

What are you doing here?

I don't know.

Do you like it here?

They are kind to me.

Look at that lamp. Beautiful—polished brass— giving out a powerful light! Nothing like that in the lodges of the Tsistsista, eh?

No.

A real bed too, with a mattress and a lot of blankets. Books to read—no books in your grandfather's lodge, are there?

No. But other things were there.

What?

Nish-Ki was there. Grandfather was there. Standing Alone was there, and I loved her as I can never love a white woman.

The spirit laughed. *Women are women, Beaver Killer. They all have breasts and a sweet spot between their legs. What matter their color?*

The lodges smelled of smoke and sweet grass and Grandfather's tobacco. It smelled of love, too, and courage, and of pride in living.

Foolish boy, the spirit taunted. *Smells, courage, pride—what do they matter? This brass lamp and a tight roof over your head are worth all the smells and courage and pride in the world! Admit it, now!*

Angry with this impertinent spirit, I cried out. The spirit became frightened and disappeared, fading into vapor and trailing out the window into the night.

It was then I heard the faint scratching at my door. It was late at night, everyone was asleep. Listening, I heard the scratching again. Was someone there? Uneasy, I went to the door and turned the handle. No one. Except—a movement caught my eye. Looking down the hall where a shaft of moonlight entered the lace curtains, I saw a shadowy figure, a beckoning hand. Rebecca!

Moving quietly, I padded down the hall and found her door open. She motioned me in, pointing to a chair. Wondering, I sat down while she stood by the window, clasping and unclasping her fingers.

"What is the matter?" I whispered.

She hurried to me, taking my hands in hers. "You are in danger here, Mr. Castor! Believe me, in *great* danger!"

It was not a white dress Rebecca wore, as I had thought, but a nightgown—a frilly white thing that shone like snow in the lamplight.

"What do you mean?" I asked.

First listening for any sound from the household, she pulled the nightgown more tightly round her neck and asked, "Do you know who Jasper Pope is?"

"Editor of the *Deseret News*," I said.

She shook her head, blond ringlets falling about her shoulders.

"Much more than that! He is head of the Sons of Dan."

"The sons of who?"

"The Sons of Dan. They are a secret organization within the church, and very powerful. No one knows how they operate, or what their authority is, except for a few men like Mr. Barley and the president. But I have heard the Danites have done murder at times, and will do it again if the needs of the church should require."

I could not help smiling. Mr. Jasper Pope was a bully and a blowhard. As for Mormon assassins, I could not think of these rosy-cheeked soberly dressed farmers countenancing any such activities.

"I'm not afraid of Jasper Pope," I said, "especially as long as Mr. Barley is my friend." But when I rose, putting my hand on her shoulder to comfort her, she shivered and drew away. "Isaac is afraid of Jasper Pope, too," she whispered. "Everyone is, and with good cause."

"Nonsense," I laughed. More to distract her than anything else, I picked up a framed and colored photograph from her bureau and asked, "Rebecca, who is this?"

The portrait was of a young girl, perhaps in her teens. The nose was aquiline and patrician, and the eyes were dark, filled with emotion. Whom did those eyes, that serious look, the delicately chiseled nose remind me of?

"Oh, bother!" she cried. "Listen to me! You have offended Mr. Pope, and he will make you pay for it! Will you not take me seriously?"

I held the portrait to the lamp, examining it closely. "I know that face," I decided. "A friend of yours?"

Angry and upset, she snatched the frame from me and threw it on the bed. "If you must know, it is my friend Julie Hazlitt, who came here with her father when he was commanding Fort Douglas but has now gone to Sacramento to live!"

I was thunderstruck. "Julie who?"

She stared at me. "Why—Hazlitt! Julie Hazlitt."

That was why I remembered those features! The tattered newspaper item my grandfather had shown me so long ago in his camp in the Iron Mountains—the picture of her father, the horse soldier Hazlitt! The same eyes, the same nose, the same cool elegant appearance!

"Do—do you know Miss Hazlitt?" Rebecca stammered.

"You were her friend," I muttered, unbelieving.

"Yes, I was, and proud to be so. Julie was a fine young lady, and her father very respected here for the good works he did."

Good works, I thought. *A butcher, a devil!* And his daughter; the devil's spawn! I kept staring at the picture on the bed until Rebecca came anxiously to me, taking my hand in hers.

"What is the matter?" she asked.

It was as if I had seen a *siyuk.* For a moment I could not speak, my throat muscles too tight and strained.

"Listen," I finally said. "Listen to me! Perhaps you are right, Rebecca. Jasper Pope does not like me, and maybe he has power to harm me. I do not care about that, because I have become used to people trying to do me harm. But I have things

197

to do, important things. Maybe it is better if I go away now anyhow, and be about these important things."

She fell back, still holding my hand, but looking at me dazedly. "Go away? Go away from—here?"

"Yes," I whispered. "I must. I have spent enough time here. Too much, perhaps."

She did not seem to understand. "Go—away? But you can't do that!"

Gently I patted her hand. Poor Rebecca! "I can," I said, "and must."

She began to cry. How can women produce tears so quickly? "But whom will I talk to?" she pleaded. "It has meant so much to me, knowing you! Just having you near is the difference between life and death in this prison!"

"Hush," I said. "You will wake the house!"

But she was not to be comforted. Wailing, she clung to my hand. "Don't go away, please! Stay here, where I can be near you!" In her emotion the nightgown became disarranged, falling over one shoulder so that the tender outline of a breast emerged through the frilly cloth. "Mr. Castor!" she pleaded. "Stay, I beg you!"

Unnerved, I tried to pull my hand away.

"Be quiet!" I whispered. "Stop crying, Rebecca!"

Though it would have been a lie, another of the long series I had been forced to tell in this white man's world, I was on the verge of agreeing to anything to stop her weeping. But I was too late.

The door banged open, quivering against the rug-wrapped brick that served as a stop. Mr. Barley stood in the doorway, majestic in his sacramental nightgown. Behind him Abigail Barley stared over his shoulder, gave a whoop of shock and disbelief, and fluttered to the floor in a swoon, the nightdress spreading around her like the plumage of a great bird shot through the heart.

"Well, I be go to hell!" Mr. Barley shouted. "What's going on here?"

It was no use trying to explain, not in those circumstances. Rebecca's window was still open, so I went through it.

CHAPTER TEN

Clawing and scrambling, I fell into a tree. For a moment I hung suspended; then a branch broke, and I fell to the ground. Flat on my back, I lay stunned. Then Mr. Barley's nightcapped head poked out the window.

"You scoundrel!" he yelled. "Come back here so I can thrash you!"

I staggered to my feet and ran. Only when I was blocks away, hidden in the trees at the edge of the square, did I stop. Panting for breath, I peeked through a screen of bushes. Street lamps lit the road with circles of yellow light. A dog slunk up, sniffed at my boots, then sneaked away.

No pursuers, at least not yet. My forehead was beaded with sweat and I wiped it with the back of my sleeve. *Heammawihio,* I thought, *am I forever to be chased like this? Must I always lie and deceive, run like a coyote?*

Nothing came back to me; no answer, no help, nothing. A night wind whipped through the square, stirring piles of autumn's leaves that still lay on the ground. Suddenly I realized I was cold. My clothes, along with the gold watch and the money Mr. Barley had given me, were in my room.

Dodging from cover to cover, I made my way back to the Barley house and hid in the shed where firewood was stacked. From there I could see the front porch, and I shivered in the darkness, wondering how I could recover my belongings.

Every lamp in the house was lit; the windows glowed with light. I could hear a bellowing noise that must have been Mr. Barley, and a great deal of hubbub and confusion.

Suddenly I jumped. In the blackness of the shed something rustled. Had I been followed? Was someone in the shadows? "Who's there?" I whispered.

No reply. Perhaps it was a rat. There were a lot of them living under the piles of firewood and old lumber. Then, hearing a commotion outside,

I peered through the warped slats of the shed.

In the light of a lantern an excited group stood on the porch, talking. Mr. Isaac Barley was there, still in his spotless nightshirt, and Jasper Pope too, with another man I had often seen with Pope; a lanky fellow with a bladelike nose and a ruff of black whiskers under his jaw. The way they were all talking at once I could not make anything out, but they were angry and indignant, that was plain to see.

I jumped again, in terror. That noise! Someone *was* in the shed! I had closed the door when I came in but now it stood open; a faint glimmer of stars shone through the opening.

"Who's there?" I called again, picking up a stick of wood. "Speak up!"

A strong hand caught my wrist, another twisted away the club.

"Me," Sanitary Sam said.

Cold sweat running off me, I sighed in relief.

"What are you doing here?" I whispered.

He spoke little English, but in the starshine I could see him nodding his head, smiling foolishly, pointing toward the porch. "Trouble," he said. "You—trouble—them."

"That's right," I agreed. "A lot of trouble. It wasn't my fault but—" I broke off. The big-nosed man had drawn a pistol from his coat and dashed down from the porch, sniffing this way and that like a hound trying to pick up a scent.

Sam saw him too, and pulled me by the arm. I followed him as he led me out of the woodshed, one bony finger to his lips, pushing me through the tangle of berry bushes behind the house. In a few minutes, skirting outbuildings and threading back alleys and thickets of brush and piles of rubbish on a hidden trail Sam seemed to know, he brought me to the UP tracks. Still holding my arm, he cupped a hand behind his ear and listened. Finally, he said, "Safe," and jabbed me in the chest, then touched his own. "You. Me. Safe."

When the early morning train chuffed out for Ogden City, I thanked Sam for his help. But he wouldn't hear of it. "Me," he protested. "With you. I be——" He wrinkled his brow, thinking. Then his face cleared. "I be go to hell," he said. "With you."

"No," I said. "You can't do that, Sam. I'm grateful, but they're chasing me. You stay here, and thank you very much."

He insisted, wrapping his rags round him with dignity, offended I should be so ungrateful. He was as scared of Pope as I myself now was, and didn't want to be abandoned to the Sons of Dan. So we both swung on an empty freight car as it rumbled past, and watched the sun come up together. In the distance lay the City of the Mormons, and beyond were the rosy tips of the Wasatch. Faintly I heard the strains of a bugle as that idiot came out and played *O Ye Mountains High, O Zion Dear Zion, Land of the Free.* Well, I was *ho nuh ka wa* again, the dedicated man. It smelled good, that clean fresh air of freedom.

If I thought Salt Lake City was impressive, Sacramento staggered me. Never had I seen so many people, so many street fights, so much wealth. It was a rough, brawling place, not at all like the businesslike bustle of Salt Lake City. The streets thronged with well-dressed people and fashionable carriages and great rumbling drays loaded with goods for the steamboats plying the river to San Francisco. Sam had a few coins in a leather bag around his neck so we bought a loaf of bread and some cheese and sat on the wharf, watching clouds of black smoke belching from the twin stacks of the *Washoe*, the *New World*, and the *Chrysopolis.*

I had underestimated Sam. Now I learned that when he was a young man, "long time back"—he waved a hand in the air—he had been all the way to San Francisco and worked on the steamers. While I munched the last of bread and cheese, he went shambling off to see if he could get a job for us. We were penniless.

I promised to meet him later, and hurried away to see if I could find my quarry—General Hazlitt. But an Army quartermaster captain, bossing the loading of bales of hay for the cavalry, told me the general had left Sacramento three months since to take command of the Western Department of the Army, headquartered at the Presidio in San Francisco.

That was a blow! Hazlitt was like the coyote, darting from cover to cover just ahead of me, now close enough to catch, almost, but bounding away again as my fingers touched his hide. *Damn it all,* I thought, *will I never be allowed to finish off this sworn business?*

I do not want to bore anyone with the time Sam and I spent in Sacramento. There is nothing exciting about it, nothing important, except one thing I will tell about later. Otherwise, Sam found an old friend who was now first mate of the *Contra Costa* sidewheeler, and that friend talked to a friend of his who got us jobs at a Sacramento woodlot run by a skinflint named Henry Jonas. All that summer we worked side by side sawing endless cords of wood and loading them on steamers that tied up at Jonas's wood yard, ramming their noses into the bank while we staggered up a ramp under loads of river oak and bull pine. Even a small steamer could burn fifty cords of wood coming upstream from San Francisco. My hands grew rough and scarred, my back screamed in protest, but Sam and I made a dollar a day. It wasn't much; by the time we paid for a miserable shack on the waterfront and enough food to blunt our bearlike appetites, little was left. Traveling to a big expensive place like San Francisco and living while I tried to find General Hazlitt would take money. And my small savings dwindled further when Sam cut his hand with an ax and a doctor charged us three dollars to sew it up. *Be patient, Grandfather,* I thought. *Like the tortoise, I seem slow. But I am very determined.*

I filled out that summer. I could feel my back muscles splitting out of the ragged shirt, my thighs bursting the seams of the old pants. Though most Indians have scant facial hair, my mustache and beard grew considerably, I suppose because of my French grandfather. I had to keep it trimmed with a jackknife.

We got to know all the boats—the *Apache*, *Modoc*, *Santa Clara*, and the rest. Sometimes, during a delay, Sam and I sneaked aboard one of the grander boats like the *New World* to marvel at the sights. Sam knew a cook on the *New World*, and Clem would covertly feed us—fresh game and fish, huge oysters, anchovies washed down with stolen wines—while we goggled at the magnificence. Prospectors, gunmen, merchants, bankers, gilded sons of Delta planters on their way to taste the delights of San Francisco; the great saloon, with Oriental carpets, crystal chandeliers, oil paintings, and potted palm trees; at one side the polished mahogany bar with six—no less than six—sleek bartenders, and a dazzling array of polished and sparkling bottles and glasses and cups and goblets. Sam and I were faint with astonishment. Once we even had to leap off the *New World* and swim for shore, having tarried too long. Perhaps my French blood gave me the curly black hair which sprouted on my chin that summer, but I suspected also it had given me an appreciation of the luxury aboard the *New World* too. I felt uneasy about it. After all, that was a white man's world, aboard the steamers, and I made up my mind not to be impressed. But something happened one day to make it easier to stay away from the boats, to forego the excitement and rich viands and fine wines Clem sneaked to us.

Sam and I were standing on the main deck of the *New World*. I was gnawing a chicken leg and Sam had just tucked a half bottle of fine liquor under his ragged coat. I had been teaching him English, and he muttered happily, "Cognac! Damn fine, you bet." Just then a military officer brushed past me with a quick, "Excuse me, young man."

It was Captain Germany, the adjutant from Fort McPherson! No, *Major* Germany now, shiny gold oak leaves on his shoulder straps. Too shaken to move, I watched him hurry down the passageway, carrying a satchel bulging with papers. Germany hadn't recognized me, and that was understandable, changing as I had in four years. But it had been a close call. I was sweating as I hurried Sam off the boat and back to the safety of the high-piled cords of wood.

"Never mind," I told Sam. "I don't want to explain. It's just that I—well, I think we've been living pretty high. We ought to stay off the boats for a while. Anyway, you're getting fat." I dug him in the paunch. "See?" I never went back on a steamer again—at least not until that stormy October day when I had to.

It had rained for three days. The skies were filled with leaden clouds that hung like curtains in the sky. Sam and I sloshed round the wood yard, building neat cords, while the other men loaded stacks of pine aboard the *Antelope*, for Captain Van Pelt. Sam was happy in the rain, feeling himself being washed clean. He always carried a bit of lye soap, and was lathering his wrinkled hide and singing as he worked. Suddenly, through the drizzle, I saw a remembered face. I froze, catching Sam's arm.

"What you do?" Sam protested.

I pointed. Mr. Jonas stood in the rain, talking to a bearded man carrying an umbrella. It was the ax-nosed fellow I had last seen on the porch of Mr. Isaac Barley's house in Salt Lake City, the one who had dashed through the yard with his pistol, looking for us; one of Jasper Pope's Danites. Sam looked, and froze too.

"Let's go!" I muttered.

We dodged behind a pile of cordwood, but the yard was fenced. There was no way out except the gate where Jonas and the Danite were talking.

"Where we go?" Sam implored. "What we do?"

Two things happened at once; two things made up our minds for us. The *Antelope* lifted the gangplank and blew her whistle, ringing a jangle of bells for "reverse engines." And the Danite rushed round the corner of the stack of logs, protecting himself from the rain with his umbrella but brandishing in the other hand the huge pistol of that spring night so long ago.

"Stand!" he bawled. "Don't move or I'll shoot! I've got a warrant for you!"

I raised my hands to reassure him, at the same time lunging out and kicking him in the groin. Sam hit him on the head with a stick of bull pine but only caught him a glancing blow so that the Danite fell to one knee, still holding the pistol.

"Stop!" he shouted, but Sam and I had gone. Slipping and sliding in the mud, we plunged into the shallows of the river and pulled ourselves aboard the *Antelope.* A shot rang out. Splinters flew from a carved and painted post by my ear. Captain Van Pelt leaned from the pilothouse overhead and bawled, "What in hell you think you're doing, you rascal, firing on my boat?"

More bells jingled; the *Antelope* turned down stream, paddles churning whirlpools as the blades bit into the current. Another shot sounded.

As I ducked I saw the Danite furious on the bank, bareheaded and without his umbrella, holding the pistol in both hands to bombard us.

A report sounded overhead, and the Danite dodged behind a pile of wood. Captain Van Pelt was shooting back. Evidently he was behind schedule on his San Francisco run and did not have time to spare except to return a few shots at our pursuer. Quickly I felt in my pocket. Remembering how I had been run out of the city of the Mormons penniless, I had taken to keeping our money with me at all times. It was there, a small sack with about ten dollars in nickels and dimes.

"Sam," I said, "wash that soap off your face and your ears. We're going to San Francisco whether we can afford it or not."

From that time on everything went wrong. Not having enough money to pay our passage, Captain Van Pelt took the ten dollars and made us work out the rest of the trip. I guess I hadn't been aware of it, but all the running and worrying and lying had told on me. Now I became very sick. It started as a bad cold in the head, taken when Sam and I worked in Jonas's wood yard. It rained downriver, and carrying cargo aboard in the October drizzle got me. They say Indians have weak lungs. I don't know if it is true, but when I began to cough hard and have a fever, I got scared, remembering the time I fled the school and traveled in the snow to Grandfather's village. I had been very sick then, and I was beginning to be sick all over again.

I got worse, finally going out of my head with fever and bone-rattling chills. Captain Van Pelt, though he wanted his fare and ordered us to work it out to the penny, relented when he saw how sick I was. He let me sleep on a pile of grain sacks and had a steward bring me hot soup which I couldn't eat. When we tied up at the Davis Street landing in San Francisco, Captain Van Pelt remembered we were without funds, and gave Sam back our ten dollars.

From then on, I don't remember much. Without Sanitary Sam, the Paiute whom I thought so low grade, I would have died. Later, piecing together my own recollections and Sam's stories, I know he took me to a place in Hinckley Alley. Sam knew Jessie Gottschalk who ran the place. She took pity on me, putting me up in a closetlike room under the eaves. "For," the red-haired Jessie wheezed, one hand under my arm helping me up the stairs and Sam steadying me with the other, "every room I got is busy." They were, too.

While I lay in bed, alternating between sleep and delirium, Sam got a job as swamper in the Bank Exchange, a saloon in Montgomery Street near California, and worked long and hard to keep us. For weeks I lay near what must have been death, but was too tired to care. Once, when each breath rattled hoarse and painful in my chest, Jessie Gottschalk called Dr. Simpson from the drugstore at Pacific and Davis. He gave me calomel pills and predicted I wouldn't last out the night. But I did. I had to. I had promised Grandfather.

Finally, the fever broke; the chills departed. Weak and exhausted, I had hardly enough strength to open my eyes. Mrs. Gottschalk told the girls, who trooped in to bring me candy and a half bottle of Pisco brandy, the sight of which made me sick all over again. But now the sickness of body was mending, sickness of the mind came on me. Once, long ago, I had ridden the paint pony up to the Slash Dollar ranch with boundless confidence. I was young and spirited, the very devil of a fellow. In fact, I was invincible; I knew it! Now I grew frightened of my own shadow. What was I doing here, in a strange room in Hinckley Alley? Even the name sounded strange and frightening. Jessie's red hair scared me, shadows in a corner of the room became Jasper Pope come to kill me, or the Pinkerton detective Laban Perkins, or even Mr. Orlo Pratt, considering his cuckolding and visiting San Francisco for a belated revenge. Desperately I wanted *Nish-Ki.* I wanted to see my grandfather's face, smell sweet grass and smoke and roast deer, see our tall lodges, hear Doll Man riding about the camp to bellow the day's news. Sweat broke out on my forehead, terror gripped me at the thought I was far from home. What vanity had brought me here? How could anyone think Beaver Killer could even exist in such a world, let alone bring an important white man to the justice of the *Tsistsista*?

In panic I cried out. One of Jessie's girls ran in from the next room but I got hold of myself and waved her away.

"Just a bad dream," I said feebly.

Falling back on the bed, I knew I was lost. My plans were ridiculous. The white men would put me in jail before I ever saw to the horse soldier Hazlitt. Sadly I remembered that there was no home for me, that my grandfather no longer had a village. The *Tsistsista* were in jail too, at Fort McPherson.

But in my depression I reckoned without *Sweet Medicine*. Great magic began to seep gradually from the *parfleche* cylinder hanging round my wasted neck. When winter came to Hinckley Alley, I had improved enough to totter down stairs to a Christmas party. In January I felt well enough to walk about a little, wrapped in a fur coat and muffler which, Jessie Gottschalk explained, had been left behind by a deadbeat customer when she threw him out of the house. In February I started to help in the kitchen. When the Negro cook argued with Jessie and got hit in the head with a skillet, he left abruptly and she asked me to take over the cooking. She paid well, and by spring I had a hundred dollars put away, in addition to some suits and a raincoat Jessie gave me. Also, my skinny body filled out; I began to look like a man again, so much so that some of Jessie's girls hung around my kitchen in their free moments and suggested I go to bed with them. Well, it had been a long time since the Slash Dollar and Madam Blanche, but I declined. Too long I had dallied, but now I was ready. *Sweet Medicine,* I said to myself, *thank you very much. Now is the time to get on with it.*

But how? It wouldn't be easy. For three dollars I bought an ancient Root's Patent .41 caliber pistol in a pawnshop on Commercial Street, and walked all the way to the Presidio to see where General Hazlitt lived. An armed Negro sentry wouldn't let me enter the grounds, since I had no legitimate business. When I asked about General Hazlitt, trying to keep my voice casual, he looked surprised.

"Ain't you heard?"

"Heard what?"

"Gin'ral done retired. Put in his thutty years and that was enough, I guess. Anyway, they had a big ceremony for him last month. It was in the newspapers."

"Where did he go?" I asked, hoping Hazlitt had not eluded me again.

The soldier scratched his woolly head. "Seems to me he running for the Legislature or some such thing."

"Then he's still here in town?"

"Oh, sho'," my informant said. "Cap'n Pickett say he visit the gin'ral last Wednesday. Lives on the Clay Street hill, in one of them big fine houses."

At the time, Sam and I were staying in a furnished room on Kearney Street. I hurried back, put on the best of the suits Jessie Gottschalk had given me, and blacked my boots.

"What in hell you do?" Sam asked, perplexed.

I couldn't tell him. I couldn't tell anyone. This was between *Sweet Medicine*, Grandfather, and me. "You keep on trying to read that book," I told him. "When you come to a word you don't know, mark it with a pencil. I'll help you later."

For days I hung round the mansion on Clay Street, loaded pistol stuck in the trousers under my coat. But there was an iron-spiked fence around the place; the street gate and carriage entrance were locked except when someone was going in or out. Once, hiding behind a tree, I saw a shiny carriage emerge, with a team of fine blacks and a liveried coachman. A cloaked figure in a plug hat sat in back, with a veiled lady at his side. But it was too far for the old Root's Patent. Anyway, I decided, that was no way to do it. Hazlitt must be killed knowing *why* he was killed! He must have time to contemplate his death and the reason for it. No sudden ambush would do. Somehow I had to work my way into that house; confront the general alone, accuse him of the great wrong he had done the *Tsistsista*, and send him to hell with certain knowledge of his sins.

Again, how? I racked my brain. Sometimes, when Sam tried to talk to me, I didn't hear him, so deep I was in contemplation. There must be a way. There *had* to be a way. My forehead became wrinkled from perpetual thought. *Si No Pah*, the kit fox! He was the cunning one. I had to be like *Si No Pah*. But when I tried to remember the words of the kit fox's song I had forgotten them. Bewildered, I tried this word and that. No good! But how could I have forgotten that song? I learned it as a child! Well, anyway, song or no song, I still had to be cunning, clever. I had to figure this out.

The solution came in an interesting way, and it didn't seem to me that *Sweet Medicine* had much to do with it. Maybe his power didn't extend to San Francisco and the Clay Street hill. But one of Jessie Gottschalk's girls had musical talent; Jessie paid for violin lessons for Ernestine at Professor Gabriel's Academy on Kearney Street. That Sunday while we were visiting Jessie, she said how well Ernestine was getting along. "But it costs me a great deal of money," she complained.

"That's a high-toned place, Gabriel's Academy. A lot of the swells sends their sons and daughters there to learn to play the fiddle or twang a harp or some such foolishness. Even Julie Hazlitt takes from the Professor, and you know what a big mucketymuck *her* father is!"

"Julie Hazlitt?" I asked, startled.

"Yep. Father's running for state senator. You know—used to be some kind of a general out at the Presidio. Big society people, but Ernestine says the daughter is just as common as an old shoe. Real nice, and handsome into the bargain, though Ernestine says Miss Julie hits a lot of clinkers on her fiddle."

Suddenly I knew how to do it! It would surely work! I needed Sam's help, but I felt he would give it. Walking back to the furnished room, I told Sam I desperately wanted to meet Miss Julie Hazlitt, that it was important for reasons I couldn't explain right then, but that I wanted his help.

"I know," Sam grinned. He gestured about. "It spring!"

"Well," I said, "maybe that's part of it."

He pointed to a bird that sat on a lacy branch, singing its heart out in the Sunday sun. "This time of year everything want to love," he said. "Even old Sam."

For a moment I felt a pang in my heart. Everything was new and green and growing, and

I must kill the horse soldier and then be killed myself. I was sworn to it, dedicated. It was sad to die at nineteen. I knew I would die; they would catch me, of course, and kill me then. But I steeled myself against such thoughts. I had come too far, seen too much, done too many things to back out now.

In our room I opened a can of beans and shared it with Sam, explaining my plan to meet Miss Julie Hazlitt. He was thunderstruck, and indignant.

"I no steal!" he shouted, wrapping the shabby coat about him and glaring at me. "Sam good Indian! What in hell, you think I steal?"

"Look," I insisted, "it's not really stealing! At the last minute, I'll grab it from you and then you run away. That's all you have to do!"

Still he refused, wagging his head and even bursting into tears, wiping his nose with a dirty rag and wailing protests. Finally I did something I was ashamed of.

"All right," I sighed. "But once Jasper Pope was caning you in Salt Lake City, and I seem to remember I saved your hide from a thrashing. It's sad to see you ungrateful now."

He trembled with fear, remembering. He was deathly afraid of Pope, and the Sons of Dan.

"Now," I said cruelly, "you refuse to help me. Oh, Sam, Sam, I *am* disappointed in you."

Still trembling, he sought for my hand and

217

pressed it against his cheek. "I do it," he muttered. "You say so—I do it." Still holding my hand, he looked at me, eyes wet with tears. "Just for you," he sniffled. "Sam owe you, Sam pay. But Sam *good* Indian."

I avoided his gaze. "Certainly," I said. "Of course you're a good Indian, Sam. And I'll be forever grateful to you."

In a way, I was glad I was going to die soon. I could not stand much more of this white man's world and the villainies I had mired myself in.

On the appointed day I dressed myself in the best I had. I had spent fifty cents for a flowered cravat, and another dollar for a fine white shirt. It was important I look prosperous. Around the comer from Professor Gabriel's Academy I again went over the plan with Sam.

"Remember," I warned, "as soon as the carriage leaves, climb into it and grab her purse. She'll probably scream, but don't let that frighten you. I'll come around the corner, and jump into the carriage too. I may have to knock you around some, but that's just for show. Then you break for it—drop the purse and run around the comer and down the alley. Go up those stairs we saw and into the tailor shop and out the front door and lose yourself in the crowd at the market."

Sam was scared; his wrinkled face was pale, but he nodded his head and muttered, "I do it!"

A few minutes before ten the carriage I had seen on Clay Street pulled up at the door of the Academy. Yawning, the driver tied the reins round the whip and went to dozing in the sun while the crowd swarmed past.

Violin lesson finished, Miss Julie Hazlitt came out on the boardwalk, raising a lacy parasol against the sun. Suddenly awake, the coachman scrambled down and handed her into the carriage. As the blacks pulled away, I signaled Sam. Now!

He was as good as his word. Loping alongside the carriage, he clambered up into it, at the same time reaching for Miss Julie's purse. She didn't scream—I had been wrong about that—but instead pulled away, trying to hold onto her purse, and belabored Sam with the parasol.

Even then, the street was so busy no one else appeared to notice the drama. Just as the driver turned round to see what the commotion was, I vaulted into the rolling carriage and dealt Sam a blow in the head with my clenched fist.

"There!" I cried. "Let go this young lady's purse, you rascal!"

Sam gave me a mortified look, clutching his ear where I had banged it. Then, remembering his role, he dropped the purse and scrambled from the carriage. The last I saw of him he was running like a rabbit, dodging in and out of the crowd, who were only now beginning to turn and stare.

"Here—here is your purse, ma'am," I stammered, "I—I—"

Still she had not spoken. Of all of us, she was the most cool and unruffled. Violet-hued eyes stared at me from the deep shade under the brim of her straw hat. For a white girl, she was the most beautiful I had ever seen.

"I am very glad," I muttered, "to have been of service to you." A crowd of curious spectators began to gather round the stopped carriage. I looked down Kearney Street, over their heads. "The rascal has got clear away," I said. "A good thing, too, or I'd have thrashed him."

When she spoke, her voice was soft and low yet very clear. It trembled only a little, and I realized she *had* been frightened, after all.

"I must thank you, sir," she said. "He might have harmed me. It was brave of you, and I thank the Lord for your help."

For a moment all hung in the balance. I began to sweat; did she see the beads on my forehead? Would this thing go further, as I had planned?

"Nothing," I said. "At any rate, nothing any man would not have done for a beautiful lady molested by a ruffian."

Suddenly everything swung my way. "I will tell Father what you have done," she decided. Rummaging in her purse, she looked for a pencil. "If you will be so kind as to tell me your name—"

Quickly I handed her one of the bogus cards I had had printed in a shop on O'Farrell Street.

"Mr. John Beaver," she said. "From Rio Vista! Father and I used to live in Sacramento, rather near there."

Easily I slid into my new identity. After all, I had done it many times before, and was by now an accomplished liar.

"Yes, ma'am," I said politely. "My father has land there. Cotton, and some wheat and corn." I had observed the gilded Delta youth that rode the *Apache* and the *New World* and the rest of the boats, and worked at cultivating their elegant way of talking. "And may I be so bold as to inquire your name, ma'am?"

She folded the battered parasol before replying. Then she said, "I am Julie Hazlitt. My father is General Hazlitt, who lately commanded at the Presidio." She extended a gloved hand. "And now thank you very much! Perhaps you will hear from us soon, Mr. Beaver. Good morning."

I stood on the walk in a daze. People brushed past me, jostled me, turned to look curiously. In the scuffle my new cravat had been pulled awry, and I reached up to straighten it, seeing again those chestnut tresses, the cool violet eyes, feeling the softness of the dainty hand in mine. As Sam had pointed out, it was spring.

When I got back to the room, Sam was holding a hot cloth to his ear. "You no have to hit so hard!" he shouted. But except to feel relief he had gotten away without incident, my mind was busy with other thoughts. For a long time I lay on the bed, hands locked behind my head, staring out the window. Night came; the western sky flushed and reddened and faded into black.

"You hungry?" Sam asked, holding out a chunk of bread torn from the loaf. "Better you eat something!"

Sunk in pleasant reverie, I waved him away. Three days later a servant delivered a note that Miss Julie Hazlitt and her father would be pleased to receive Mr. John Beaver of Rio Vista at their home on Clay Street at 3 P.M. of a Sunday. There would be a musical gala.

CHAPTER ELEVEN

General Wesley E. Hazlitt, USA (Retired), was a small man with a grimacing red face above a pepper-and-salt beard, as it was called. He prowled among the guests still in Army blue with starred shoulder straps, shaking hands, laughing, gesturing with a cigar. Miss Julie Hazlitt moved on his arm in a high-bodiced gown, dark hair done up in a knot atop her head.

"And this—" she said, pausing before me. "Papa, this is the young man I told you about. Mr. John T. Beaver, from up the river at Rio Vista."

Puffing hard on the cigar, the general took both of my hands in his, shaking them hard. I must admit to trembling at this touch of the devil. "So you're the young man who saved my Julie, eh? Damn fine thing you did, sir! I'm forever grateful to you. Cotton, eh? Your father, I mean."

"Yes, sir," I murmured.

"Need cotton!" General Hazlitt barked. "Clothes the nation, that's what! Nothing more important, eh? When I get to the Legislature, I mean to come out for preferential shipping rates for cotton growers." He dug me in the ribs and laughed, a deep rumble for so small and badgerlike a man. "Tell your pa that when you go back to Rio Vista!" With a quick jerk of his head he turned to Miss Julie. "Dear, do you remember any family named Beaver when we were up in that country?"

She pursed her lips in thought while I stood helpless, not knowing what to say. I had lived among white people now for several years, and learned a few of the social graces, but I was nevertheless a very young man, brash and bumbling. The great house and its guests scared me. Would I say the right thing? Or would some careless word betray me? But there was no need for concern. The general squeezed my arm, baring tobacco-stained teeth in a quick grin, and trotted toward another group. Miss Julie cast me an apologetic smile and was gone too; a tall beautiful woman on the arm of this brusque man who snorted about like a high-pressure boiler ready to blow. A soldier he was, certainly; every move showed the quick and sure way of a man used to commands and decisions. But he was a clever politician, too. He would certainly go to the Legislature if it were not for John T. Beaver of Rio Vista or whatever I was now calling myself. Sometimes it was hard to remember.

Later, I sat among some potted palms trying not to hear a fat lady sing a song called *A Flower from My Angel Mother's Grave*. At long last, I had met the devil. Years of remembering his misdeeds and seeing the face in the faded clipping had made him grow in my mind to giant's stature. Still, while General Hazlitt did not look so impressive as I expected, he was yet the devil. Bad things come in small as well as large packages. However, about the devil's spawn, Miss Julie, my feelings were mixed up, and I ran my finger nervously round the unaccustomed tight collar. Could Julie be blood of the devil, bone of his bone, and not be stained by his misdeeds? She loved him, that was easy to see from the way she looked at him, pride in her eyes as she passed on his arm among their guests. Even as they finished the round of greetings and came near again, she whispered to him with a pat on the arm, "Now, Papa, try to calm yourself a little! The evening has just started, and you must not get so excited."

It was like a mother tenderly restraining a child.

When she came to take the seat I offered, the violet eyes still followed as he trotted off toward a group of old friends.

"He *will* drive himself so," she sighed, opening the painted fan and sweeping it through the air, "and at his age it isn't good for him. I beg him and beg him to rest, now he has left the Army! But politics is his new love. He works almost harder at it then he did at being a soldier. Every day I live in fear he will suffer a fit of apoplexy."

There was a scent of flowers about her, a smell of spring blooms to match the color of her eyes. For lack of anything better to say, I stammered, "You—you and your father seem to have many friends."

The violet eyes saddened. "They are for the most part his friends, not mine! Leading citizens, old Army cronies—after Mama died, I lived with Papa in Army post after Army post, never staying long enough to make friends—at least not the enduring kind of friend a girl wants and needs."

So far from home, so friendless also (except for Sanitary Sam), I felt I knew her loss. On sudden impulse, I bent over her hand and kissed it.

"Miss Julie," I said, "perhaps I can become that kind of friend to you, and you to me."

Her eyes suddenly misted with tears, and she spread the fan over her mouth to conceal her feelings. After a moment she murmured, "Why, that is very kind of you, Mr. Beaver! God willing, I hope it will be so."

Spring in San Francisco is a lovely season. Trees greened into leaf, in the parks flowers bloomed, a fresh clean breeze laden with the smell of salt whipped the bay. The skies were intense blue broken only by puffy wisps of cloud. I had not forgot my mission—at least I thought about it from time to time—but the days passed so swiftly I had not yet planned how I would confront General Hazlitt alone. Always he was surrounded by people; he loved to be in the midst of friends, haranguing them about politics. He became very tired, and often dozed on a settee at a late dinner party. But a moment later, refreshed, he would bound to his feet and join the guests. Julie was right—politics was his life.

Now I was invited often to the big house on Clay Street. Julie and I took walks in the garden, and became friends. In a book store on Stockton Street I had bought a dog-eared copy of *Miss Agatha's Compendium of Etiquette for Young Ladies and Gentlemen*, and memorized at least half of it.

"But you must have many other gentlemen," I said teasingly, holding her arm and bending to pass under a skein of candlelit Japanese lanterns.

She laughed. Though I had found out she was twenty-one, almost two years older than I, she had a delightful childlike way about her. "Have you seen them?" she demanded. "Are they not a ragtag and bobtail collection? Simpering young dandies, without a brain in their heads!" In a corner of the garden where a flowering vine made scented shadows, she shook her head ruefully. "No, thank you, Mr. Beaver! I have no time to waste on them."

I was beginning to act foolish, and knew it. Hoping for a compliment, I said, "But I am no better. What ever can you see in me, I wonder?"

This time there was no laughter. She gripped my arm, staring long and hard into my face. I could see in her dark eyes the reflected glow of the paper lanterns.

"You are different," she said. "There is something about you that tells of depth, great depth; a kind of—well, purpose, integrity, maturity. I know it in my soul, Mr. Beaver. I can not explain it, nor do I care to. It is enough that God has made you so." Unnoticed by me, she stripped off the long white glove. Suddenly her fingers stroked my lips. "You are my friend," she murmured. "I do not think I have ever quite had such a friend."

The touch of flesh startled me. But the moment was gone. Laughing, she got to her feet, tugging at my arm. "Papa will be furious we were gone so long," she said. "Perhaps we had better join the rest."

Later, in the rented room Sam and I shared on

Pacific Street, I confronted the awesome reality of my situation. I was beginning to show signs of infatuation with an innocent young girl, at the same time planning to kill her father! What had come over me? Was it love? No, of course not! How could I love the daughter of such a devil? Infatuation, that was all it was! Restlessly I tossed and turned on my bed till Sam awoke, grumbling, to scold me.

"I'm sorry," I said, and tried to sleep again, but Sam would not let me.

"Wake up!" he growled, face covered with soapsuds. "Sam got to work. Bread and cheese on table, coffee in pot."

My social life now took most of my time. Sam had found work in an iron foundry to support us; I had used all my money and had to borrow frequently from him, to buy clothes and other things I needed, but kept an accounting and meant to pay him back.

"Can you let me have five dollars?" I asked.

He shook his head, fumbling in his pocket to bring out a purse. "God damn!" he complained. "Take all my money, you!"

"Thanks," I said. "You're a good friend."

When Sam was gone I yawned my way out of bed and poured coffee. I had been late last night, very late, joining Julie and her father's friends at a champagne supper in Montgomery Street. In a detached way I was still the dedicated

228

man, and soon would give my life to avenge the *Tsistsista*. But right now I was entitled to enjoy myself, at least for a while. I had gotten to enjoy their food, the sparkle of French champagne, candlelit oyster suppers, walks in the garden with Julie. I spent each day in danger, that was true. While no one appeared to question my Rio Vista story, there was always a possibility some slip, a thoughtless action, would give me away. The *parfleche* cylinder lay in my bureau drawer on Pacific Street; I would take no chances of having to explain it to someone. Wrapped in an oiled cloth, the Root's Patent pistol lay beside it. Some day soon, I would consult the one, and use the other. But now I was to meet Julie and go shopping.

At eleven I waited in the lobby of the Excelsior Hotel among splashing fountains and potted greenery. To conceal the fact that I lived in a shabby rooming house, I gave out that I had rooms at the Excelsior. For a small bribe to the desk clerk, I received messages there. It was a dangerous stratagem; so far it had worked.

But what Julie said that morning shocked me; my face betrayed it.

"You are to come for dinner tonight," she told me. "Papa is having a group of men in to discuss the plight of the Indians."

"The—Indians?" I blurted.

"Why, whatever is the matter with you,

John?" she asked, concerned. "You—you look so *strange!*"

"Nothing," I lied. "Nothing at all. A dizziness, perhaps, from late hours. But—Indians?"

"The California Indians," she explained. "Poor wretches—they are miserable, living in hovels and eating snails and rats and such. I have insisted Papa do something for them when he is in the Legislature."

The California Indians! For a moment I had feared the matter bore somehow on me.

"Papa especially wants you to be there," she went on. "He has taken a liking to you, John, and I am so happy. He too thinks you a remarkable young man; very wise and dignified, and with prospects in politics also, if you should choose."

It was ironic; General Wesley E. Hazlitt doing something for Indians, even California Indians!

"Then you will come?" she asked.

I touched her gloved hand with my lips. "I shall be delighted," I said.

The discussion after dinner that evening was spirited. The ladies withdrew, and I sat in a chair near the wall, pretending to smoke a large cigar which was sure to make me sick, and sipping brandy moderately lest it loosen my tongue. The general was in fine fettle.

"There is no limit to the progress this great nation can make," he was saying. "With a fine Republican like Mr. Arthur in the White House, it is time for the various states to assert their proper roles in our Federal Union. The time for massive national action is past; now the states must take over, acting vigorously to meet the problems within their own boundaries."

Like my grandfather, the general was a natural orator, though limited in poetry and sweep of feeling, as my grandfather was not.

"I don't know," a whiskered man in iron-rimmed spectacles said, pulling at his beard. "The national situation is still unsettled, General. Banks are overextended, credit is tight; mark my words, we're in for a squall!"

There was a lot of similar talk, very boring. The Negro servant brought more brandy, and cigars. I declined the latter, but took more brandy. The conversation eventually got around to the California Indians—the Yokuts and Chumash and Diegueños. I had seen some in the city, and they were poor specimens, worse than the Paiutes of the Utah Territory. But as the talk went on, I became annoyed. Perhaps it was the brandy. At any rate, I fidgeted in the corner as the general outlined his plans for Indian relief. They might have been discussing dogs, or cattle, or goats; not people. These men had no feeling in them, no feeling at all, for the poor creatures as living breathing humans, with all the fears and loves and passions of man. Finally General Hazlitt turned to me, saying, "Many of you know Mr.

Beaver. He is a friend of my daughter Julie, and a young man with a good head on his shoulders. Sir, what do you think of my proposition?"

"With great respect, sir," I said, "I do not think very much of it."

Silence fell on the group. General Hazlitt blinked in surprise. At his elbow a grizzled major, a former companion in arms, tugged at his mustache, muttering. But the general was fair-minded. With a lifted hand he stilled the whispers, and said, "Perhaps we are too inbred, we politicians. A fresh viewpoint may help. Will you explain, sir?"

"What strikes me," I said, "is that you all speak of depots and barracks and communal dining halls as if Indians were one group, to be handled and kneaded like a vat of dough, to be sliced into chunks and baked in an oven and come out brown and still and peaceful. But Indians— even California Indians—are men, and women, and children. This kind of treatment is bound to degrade them in heart and mind and spirit. They live on their own lands, theirs by right of thousands of years tenancy. By what law does the white man seize their lands and force them into barracks?"

Caught up in my own arguments I rose to my feet, gesturing with the cigar. "I am young," I went on, "and do not have the wisdom of my elders. But I have a feeling for people they do not have. Look at the Sioux, and the Cheyenne; the Arapaho and the Crow. Look at them today, fenced in and broken in spirit, living on the dole! These people had a tradition, a religion, a culture that was honest and good and true. They could have given a lot to the nation. It is not yet too late, if men of understanding and good will take action to help. But the way to help Indians is not with stockades and fences and communal barracks, but with title to their own lands; perhaps with money to buy cattle and pigs and goats if that is the only way they can exist in this white man's world." I paused for breath, laying down the cigar. "That," I said, "is the way to help any people—not alone the Indians."

No one spoke. The grandfather's clock in the corner ticked slow and loud, brass pendulum swinging to and fro, each passage marked by a glint of light reflected from the overhead lamp.

"By God, sir!" the grizzled major protested. "I—"

"Wait a minute, Reynolds," General Hazlitt interrupted. "I think Mr. Beaver has touched on something we ought to take into account."

A fat man in a frock coat stood up. "But that's all nonsense, sir! We can't—"

"I say it makes sense," the general insisted, "and good sense! Where's our humanity, eh? We're not dealing with sacks of beans or sides of beef, are we? John Beaver's right!" He rose, taking my hand. "By George, sir," he said, "that was eloquent! Such understanding for the poor wretches, such compassion! Now wherever did you get ideas like that, and learn to speak them so well?"

His hand lay like a smoldering brand in my palm. For a moment I thought I must cry out in pain and anguish. This was the man who ruined my people! He had killed the *Tsistsista*, and now was shaking me by the hand!

"Seems to me," Major Reynolds grumbled, "he talks like some of the damned Cheyenne and Sioux we fought in the Black Hills, General. Same way of palavering—" He tugged again at his mustache. "By the Lord Harry, young man, you even look like one of 'em! Use your hands just like they did!"

"Nonsense!" General Hazlitt laughed. "He's from Rio Vista, Reynolds—son of a cotton planter up there. But bright as a dollar, you can see that! Shook you up, did he? Well, maybe that's what us old fogies need!"

With a muttered excuse I hurried away. In the conservatory I wiped my brow, breathing deep and slow to calm my heart. I had had a narrow escape, that was true. But something deeper, more profound, shook me to the bone. Was that true, all I had said? Were they *my* people I was defending? Who *were* my people now? For so long I had been away from the *Tsistsista*. For so long had I known only white faces, and white ways, drunk white man's wines, eaten his food, spoken his tongue and worn his high collars and practiced his graces. Now who was I? I should hate them all; once I had done so! But I thought of faces—Mr. Orlo Pratt, Captain Germany the adjutant, Isaac Barley, the golden-haired Madam Pratt and her insatiable appetites. I thought of poor lonely Rebecca Barley, and Sergeant Garrity, and especially of Julie Hazlitt. Good and bad, kind and cruel, well-meaning and devious— they were as varied as the *Tsistsista*. But they had been kind to me, most of them. Who, in God's name, *were* my people?

There, I had said it! In *God's* name! Julie went to church of a Sunday, and called frequently on her God. Now I was calling on him too! Where was *Sweet Medicine*? What had happened to *Heammawihio*, The Great One Above? And for that matter, where was Standing Alone, the girl I loved? I had always meant her to be my woman someday; yet now I was infatuated with a white girl!

Trembling with emotion, I paced among the lush earth-smelling plants. In the dim light a spider fell from a fan-shaped palm, and I struck at it in terror. Everything was all mixed up. "Help me," I muttered. I did not know whom I was asking for help, but someone, something, some spirit had to help me.

"John?"

It was Julie, rustling through the gloom in her white gown.

"There you are! What a shock you gave me! Papa said you had left!"

"No," I sighed. "I'm here. I'm still here."

She touched my arm, sounding surprised. "Why, you're shaking! And pale, too! Aren't you well?"

When she withdrew her hand, I caught it and pulled it back, "I am sick," I said. "Very sick! But it's not of the body. More of the mind! A churning is going on in my heart, and I don't know how it is going to come out."

She sat beside me on the marble bench, and I could feel her thigh, her shoulder, close to mine. In the dimness of the conservatory her face shone palely. Her breath was clear and sweet on my cheek, like the breath of a baby.

"Can you not tell me what it is?"

I shook my head. A personal matter. I must wrestle with it myself.

Now her body trembled too. I could feel it through the silken sheath. But she made no move to withdraw from the intimate contact. She inclined her head toward me, the violet eyes dark pools against the pale cheeks. "If you love me," she said in a low voice, "as I think you do, you must let me share your troubles, John." The curve of her bust pressed against my arm. "You *do* love me, don't you?"

So confused and desperate I did not know what I was doing, I put one hand at the small of her back, pressing her against me. "I could not help loving you," I muttered.

Suddenly she lay against me, lips groping for mine. "I knew it," she murmured. "Tell me again, dearest. Say it again."

"I love you," I repeated. My other hand rested on her silken thigh, and it came alive under my touch. "I do not have a will of my own any more," I whispered into the hair at the nape of her neck. "I am not even a person any more. I am nothing. But I do love you. And you are all that matters to me, Julie!"

There was a thump as the conservatory door banged open. "Julie?" the general called. "Are you out there? Did you find young Beaver?"

Quickly she pulled herself away, stroking her dark hair into order.

"Yes, Papa!" she called back. "We're right here! We'll be out in a moment!"

He hesitated, then grumbled, "Well, hurry, girl! Our guests are leaving!"

At the door she paused and looked up at me, holding my face in her hands. "I love you too," she said simply. "I love you more than any man I have ever seen, except perhaps Papa, and the Lord, and that is of course something different.

For so long I have been lonely, and now it is as if I have everything I will ever need from the world."

Unsteadily I held aside the greenery. Julie stepped through the door ahead of me, into the wink of lights, the sparkle of linens, the clink of bottles. Something tremendous had happened to me, but I did not quite know what it was.

The general planned a party to remember the time the whites won their freedom from the English. They celebrated it every year on the Fourth of July. He and Julie invited over two hundred people—the mayor, aldermen, Army officers, prominent bankers, lawyers, judges, whatever. Julie said there would be fireworks (which I had never seen), a brass band, even a cannon from the Presidio with a crew to bang off a hundred and seven rounds; one for every year since their Declaration of Independence. The general ordered barrels of beer, a drink I never learned to like, along with roasted oxen and all manner of things to eat and drink. It was also an opportunity for the general to campaign for the Legislature. He never forgot politics.

Julie kept me hanging bunting, arranging tables in the garden, clearing a space next the stables for the cannon and the gun crew from the Presidio. With her father's approval, she had one of the maids clean and furnish an empty room at the back of the house for me to stay while we were preparing for the Fourth.

The general himself was not able to help with getting ready, being scheduled for several speaking engagements. He was gone a lot, often several days at a time, to visit Fresno, Red Bluff, or Sacramento. Julie's Aunt Carrie, an old woman who lived out in the Western Addition, came to stay as chaperone when the general left. But she wore thick glasses and could not see more than a few feet ahead. Julie and I had our freedom, and made use of it.

One Sunday I went to church with Julie. She was very religious; a Baptist, I think, or something like that. The church was noisy, with loud singing and praying. Their God must have been deaf. I was scared, never having been in a church. When Julie had asked me my faith, I didn't know what to say. "My father," I finally explained, "was not very religious. On Sundays we used to take the dogs and go hunting."

She laughed and kissed me. Aunt Carrie, waiting at the door, turned thick glasses toward us. "Then," Julie decided, "it is time you gave thought to your immortal soul, John. I always thought there was something of the heathen about you. Today we must call the attention of the Lord to your benighted condition."

Julie was a remarkable girl, even by *Tsistsista* standards. Brave (she had shown that in the purse-snatching), loving (how could that be doubted?), reverent (to her God, that is), clever (I could not understand why she could not see through me), and other good things. But she still had an innocent little-girl way that at times annoyed me, most of the time delighted. I think it was because of a long motherless condition on the Army posts, moving here and moving there, without a chance to make good and lasting friends. From an early age she had to make a home for her father. Perhaps, in an unknowing way, she resented the loss of a childhood, and now clung to a remnant of it. At times I urged my *Tsistsista* blood to rejoice at seducing the loved and only daughter of the devil Hazlitt. But I could not keep myself in that frame of mind. I loved her; that was the simple and desperate truth.

That evening the general called me to his study. He slumped at his desk, military tunic open at the collar, puffing a cigar. His face looked pale, almost gray, but he was brisk enough.

"Damned long day," he barked. "I'll be glad when this campaign is over. Takes a lot out of a man." He motioned me to a chair. "A few things I've been wanting to talk about to you, John."

"Yes, sir," I said, sitting on the edge of my chair. What in the world did he want to discuss? But he only smiled, knocking the ash from his cigar into a bleached buffalo-skull he kept as an ashtray. "Mentioned plans for the Indians at my speech in Sausalito. Went over well. You know, sometimes people think we military men are puppets, doing what we're ordered to do with no regret or compassion. But that isn't true. We have feelings, damn it all! I think those people in Sausalito got a different picture of me, one that may help at election time."

"I'm glad, sir," I said.

He looked at me from under the bushy brows, rolling the cigar between his fingers. "I'm grateful to you, John, for showing me that side of the coin. And I am everlastingly astonished at the depth of your feeling for the Indians. I must admit my own campaigns against the Sioux and Cheyenne were sometimes cruel. Perhaps we did not do the right thing by them. I often had misgivings, but you understand I was under strict orders! I had the safety of my own men and the settlers to think of, too. But you seem so familiar when speaking of Indians. Have you known any?"

I hesitated. Then I said, "No, not actually. But I've read a lot about their problems. I think I see what is the real issue."

He nodded, puffing the cigar into a glowing coal. "It does you credit, young man. Maybe some day I can reward your compassion for them."

"I want no reward," I said, surprised.

He seemed not to have heard me. Instead, he pressed fingers against his forehead as if it pained. "This other matter—I haven't brought it up till now, though I've thought about it a great deal." He stubbed out the cigar and stood up, hands in pockets. "What are your intentions toward my daughter?"

I could only stand there, mouth gaping like a hooked fish. But he took it for a young man's embarrassment at talk of his beloved. Chuckling, he caught me by the arm and paced about the room.

"Don't think I haven't noticed what's going on, young friend! I haven't seen my Julie so happy and radiant for a long time! Ah, it's good to hear her singing again, laughing all through this old house!" Suddenly he stopped to face me, looking hard into my eyes. "She's chosen a fine young man, I'll say that! But there's something yet to be done."

"What—what, sir?" I stammered.

"Soon I'll be going up the river to Colusa for a speech," the general said. "I think I'll stop off at Rio Vista and have a talk with your father. Any objections?"

I swallowed hard. "No, sir," I said.

"Judge Kelleher lives near Rio Vista. I'll stop in and see him first. Your father must have known the judge."

"Yes, sir," I lied. "They were fast friends."

The general squeezed my arm. "Good! I'll have the judge take me over in his trap. We'll have a drink together, the three of us, and a little talk."

In response to his curt nod, I left the room. Now what to do? Something like this had to happen, but I was taken by surprise. I only hoped the general had not noticed my nervousness.

During the next few days I wandered about bewildered and uncertain. I remembered my purpose, certainly; I knew what brought me to the mansion on Clay Street. But *Sweet Medicine* had not warned me about the complications. My brains seemed to have turned to mush; even the simplest decision was too hard. Julie noticed my behavior. Even Aunt Carrie tried to press a spoonful of patent medicine on me, crying, "Swallow it down! Got ipecac and bark and roots in it! Boys needs it every year about this time to clean out their systems!"

I needed more than Dr. Schimpf's Mediterranean Elixir. I was lost, and nothing would save me. Running away would mean abandoning my vow; staying would entrap me in the web of lies I had spun. And time, the inexorable time, the concept that always meant so little to the *Tsistsista*, was spinning itself out to fashion a noose for me.

Obstinately, though, I decided to stay on for a

while. To abandon Julie was more than I could stand. And the general had not yet gone to Colusa. Something, I thought desperately and foolishly, *must* intervene to save me.

CHAPTER TWELVE

When the glorious Fourth came, people—thousands of them, it seemed—swarmed through the house, the gardens, the conservatory. Beer flowed from chilled kegs; sides of beef, dark and crusted with basting sauce, turned slowly over beds of glowing coals; the band played military marches. At ten in the evening the cannon began their booming.

"Goodness!" cried Julie, putting her hands over her ears. "Such a racket! I wish this was 1783 instead of 1883!"

They kept me busy greeting guests, pouring champagne for the more important, carving slices of beef for the ladies, finding the fireworks man who had already gotten drunk on lager beer and had to be sobered with black coffee. When the last guest had left, the general and I stood on the veranda, looking at the welter of napkins, cups, spilled food, empty beer glasses. A rack of fleshless bones hung blackening over the embers. The band had long ago packed its instruments and clattered beerily back to the post in a rented wagon. Silvery-gray in the moonlight, a pall of woodsmoke lingered in the air. Julie and Aunt Carrie had gone inside, to freshen up after the exhausting evening.

"Well," the general sighed, "it was quite a party, eh, son?"

"Yes, sir," I said. "They all seemed to enjoy it."

"Made a few converts." The general sounded tired. "Every vote counts, just as every bullet once counted." Suddenly he swung toward me, jabbing a chewed cigar at my chest. "Oh, by the way, that reminds me!"

"Of what, sir?" I asked.

"Knowing your regard for Indians, I wanted to share a bit of news. Nothing earth-shaking, but it saddened me. I was talking to one of the reporters on the *Call* tonight, and he told me our Indian troubles on the frontier are at an end. Did you ever hear of a Cheyenne named Strong Left Hand?"

Hardly trusting myself to speak, I said, "Yes, sir, I believe I have. A chief, is he not?"

The general took a deep puff of his cigar and looked down at the red eye of the coal. "A chief, indeed. Remarkable man. One of their great leaders, to look at it from this day and this perspective. Well, Strong Left Hand was about the last of the troublemakers. They'd put him in jail at Fort McPherson, out in Nebraska. Tried to escape a week ago, but they shot him dead."

Grandfather? Dead? My heart split in two.

"Not necessary at all," the general was saying. "No need for it, really." He went on and on, meaningless syllables I recollected only later. "Now he'll be a martyr, I suppose. But the old man was a firebrand, even to the day he died. There's some talk one of his own people shot him. An Indian policeman who didn't like the way the old man kept stirring up the Cheyennes and making trouble for the few that strung along with the Army."

I was glad it was dark on the veranda so the general couldn't see the grief on my face. Grandfather murdered! While I had been living a luxurious and pampered life, *he* had not forgotten. To the end he struggled for the *Tsistsista*. I remembered what he so often told me. *A chief must always do good things. He must not think of himself. He should give horses and presents to people, and live in an honest and true way, always ready to give anything, even his life, to make things better for the people.* My cheeks burned in shame. *Beaver Killer,* I thought, *you have become rotten clear through, like a fish dead on the bank for a week.*

"Eh?" asked the general. "What was that you said, son?"

Maybe in my emotion I had muttered something. I didn't know. I didn't even care.

"Nothing," I said. "I don't believe I spoke. I—I was just thinking."

He took my hand. "Didn't mean to upset you, young man! It was a great miscarriage of justice for that old man to die so."

I couldn't stand it any longer. With an abrupt excuse I hurried away, leaving him standing on the veranda, staring after me in perplexity.

All right, Grandfather, I said to myself, once I was in my room at the back of the house. *All right. I will do it. It has taken me a long time to come to my senses. I have followed false trails. I have let myself be turned from the true path. But now is the time. Tonight look down to see your grandson fulfill the oath he took in the Medicine Lodge.*

Probably I would die tonight, myself. Because of the size of the celebration, the San Francisco police had furnished two armed officers to keep order and park carriages; I heard them below in the kitchen, drinking beer with the servants and laughing. But I didn't care. At last I was free; free of deceit and lies and pretending, free to be myself. I was Beaver Killer again, a man of the *Tsistsista.* Singing softly the kit fox song, I paced about my tiny room, crafty and quick like *Si No Pah,* making my plans.

The general always lay for a time in bed before sleeping. He read, saying this rested him, helped him relax from the strains of the day. Now what weapon? With dismay I remembered I had left the old Root's Patent pistol in my drawer in Pacific Street. Well, I would have to use something else. Maybe a knife from the kitchen, or an ax from the stables. The grooms had gone to bed.

Approaching the general's room through the hall was unwise; I might meet someone there, draw suspicion. Going to my window, I looked into the moonlight. By craning my neck I could see along the narrow balcony that joined the upper rooms of the Clay Street house. It did not extend to my small cubicle, but I could easily swing over and climb up on it, passing thus to the general's room. His glass-windowed doors were open to catch the breeze, and the curtains shimmered with a glow from the bedside lamp. But I must hurry.

Light-footed, I made my way down the back stairs. The police were still in the kitchen. On a shelf in the stables I found a small hatchet. Weighing it in my hand, I suddenly laughed to myself, delighted. There, ranged about the walls, was a collection of old buckets of paint the grooms used to spruce up carriages. Red and white and gold, green and purple. Before I confronted the devil I would paint myself in *Tsistsista* colors, so there would be no mistaking who I was.

In my room I stripped, wrapping only a ragged towel about my loins. By candlelight, with shades drawn, I crouched before the mirror, dipping my fingers into the cans and painting strokes of red and yellow and purple across my cheekbones, my chest, my arms and shoulders. I had left *Sweet Medicine* in the drawer with my pistol on Pacific Street, but I prayed to him anyway. *Watch me, Sweet Medicine, what I do. I paint myself as I go to war. By my vow in the Medicine Lodge, I dedicate myself to kill this devil so our people will again become great and respected, so they again walk proudly, kill their own food, live in their own lodges.*

The words, I was astounded to notice, were Cheyenne. They came awkwardly, unfamiliar, but made me feel good. I had not spoken that tongue for a long time. It was like coming home, like seeing *Nish-Ki*, feeling her hand on my cheek after a hard day playing the hoop game.

Now, I said to myself, *I am ready.*

Silently I went through the window. I jumped across the gap to the railing of the balcony and poised for a moment, looking round, hatchet in my hand. *Nothing. No one.* The moonlight was empty. Only a faint sound of giggling from the kitchen below.

In the shadows of the trees overhanging the balcony, I approached the open door of General Hazlitt's room. Peering through the curtains, I saw him in bed. He was in his nightshirt, a peaked cap on his head. Iron-rimmed spectacles glinted in the lamplight; he turned a page slowly, at the same time yawning.

My bare feet making no sound in the Turkey carpeting, I slipped into the room. Slowly I approached, hatchet held high. If he turned his head and saw me, I must not strike too soon. He would cry out in terror at seeing a painted warrior from the long-ago Washita. But I would shout him down. I would call out the name of Strong Left Hand, my grandfather, and I would summon *Heammawihio* himself to witness as I struck.

The pages of his book rustled as he dropped it. His eyes widened as he caught sight of me. A hand fumbled at his reading glasses. He dropped them, too.

"What—what—" he muttered, one hand searching for the spectacles.

He screwed up his eyes, blinking, and saw me standing by his bed. He drew back, face pale. "What the hell!" he said. "Who—"

Suddenly I believe a kind of realization came on him. I do not think he ever saw me as John Beaver. That was not what I wanted, anyway. But he did see in me a terrible scene in the past; the Washita, bearskin-coated troopers splashing through the shallows, the sound of guns and the cries of women and children as they ran from lodges to turn the creek red with their blood.

"Strong Left Hand," I cried out, "has come to kill you for what you did to the *Tsistsista*!"

I raised the hatchet and he writhed in alarm. Desperately he threw up one arm to fend off the blow. The grizzled face turned pale, a pallor against which the eyes swelled in disbelief.

"No!" he cried, clutching at his throat. The word was soft and muffled, as if his throat were constricted by fear. "No!" he repeated. "Go back—go back—"

My arm had started the downswing when I suddenly checked it, wondering. The eyes were still wide and staring. But his hand, the hand that had caught at his throat, suddenly dropped limp. For a moment the general's body froze in that stiff mold; then it toppled, falling sidewise and down so that he lay across the coverlet, head and shoulders drooping over the side of the bed. The military beard stuck into the air; the eyes still stared, glassy and fearful, at the flowers on the papered ceiling.

Astonished, I looked at him. What had happened? Remembering *Si No Pah*, fearing a trap, I went round the bed and approached him. Had he fainted? Perhaps, but his eyes were still open.

"What is the matter with you?" I muttered.

Kneeling, I touched his cheek. No response. Then I slapped him. "Wake up!" I insisted. "I am going to kill you!" He didn't move. Half off the bed, the upper part of his body swung gently to and fro with the force of my slap.

Could this be? The devil was dead! Feeling

cheated, I got to my feet. How could this be? I come to kill him, to cleanse the blood from the *Mahuts*, the Sacred Arrows. Now this devil, this clever devil, had outwitted me!

Looking down at the ashen face, now in strong relief from the slanting rays of the Argand lamp, I felt tears come to my eyes. What *mohin* followed me, traced my footsteps, hung at my heels to trick and deceive me? What hairy monster clung to my back, weighing me down, making me do foolish things and causing everything to come to naught? Furious, I kicked out. My bare foot caught the dead man in the mouth. As if in laughter at my failure the mouth dropped open, smiling upside-down. Panic-stricken I rushed out the window, along the balcony, and cowered in my own room.

Silence; nothing but my own heavy breathing. From below I heard the policemen taking a drunken farewell of the cook and kitchen maids. Then there was a massive stillness, the quiet of a house going to sleep after a celebration. Straining my ears, I heard the ticking of the grandfather's clock in his study somewhere below. That, and the moonlight coming in the window; that was all there was. Bitterly I sat on my cot, weeping. It had come to this. This, too, was all there was.

The funeral was big, carriages lining Market Street for blocks. A black horse headed the procession, the general's boots hanging reversed from the saddle. Later, the lawyers came to the house to read the will. After her first deep grief, Julie was dry-eyed and composed, serene in her Baptist faith; but Aunt Carrie simply dissolved into tears, sobbing, "I told him! I told Wesley all the time! Apoplexy ran in the family, I told him! But he wouldn't listen!"

At the reading of the will another bitter trick was played on me. The general left the sum of one thousand dollars to Mr. John T. Beaver of Rio Vista, ". . . in recognition of his interest in and respect for the maltreated Indian peoples of this land; the sum to be used by him in any way he deems proper for the relief of Indian afflictions and grievances."

Hardly believing I heard aright, I clenched my fists. A thousand dollars! He could not buy his way into a white man's heaven, least of all through me!

Later, in the conservatory, Julie was concerned about my strange behavior. "Is something the matter?" she asked. "You are so pale!"

Helpless and frustrated, I looked down at her. Was this the last joke to be played on me? Or was it the beginning of a strange and cunning revenge?

"I can't talk about it now," I said. "Later, perhaps—"

Never had I been so torn. Seeing her gentle worried face, I wanted nothing so much as to love her for the rest of my life. But a gulf yawned between us, a gulf so wide that *Man Hik*, chief of all birds, could never fly across.

She laid her head against my shoulder. "You do not feel well," she said. "Perhaps it is something I have done, and I am sorry. But you need never justify yourself to me, dear friend. I love you too much to ask that."

My heart was so full I could not speak. I only stood there, feeling the dark hair touch my cheek, the body warm and soft against mine. My eyes filled with tears, and I brushed them angrily away. What, then, had I become? Weeping—a man weeping? A *Tsistsista*, weeping before a woman? How could a *Tsistsista* so weep?

One winter day I woke up in a Mexican fandango house in Sullivan Alley. When I had rushed out of the house on Clay Street I never went back, never saw Julie Hazlitt again, except once, distantly, riding in a carriage on Market Street. Instead, I drank up most of the thousand dollars in parlor houses; the Rosebud, the Cock of the Walk, the House of Blazes. I was frightened. I wanted to go home. But where was home? I didn't know, but I had to go. I felt I must get away from this place or die.

I got up and ran from the building. Sam still lived in Pacific Street. I had less than a hundred dollars left from the legacy. I put the money on his bureau, after writing a few words on the back of the envelope. *This will keep you in soap for a long time. You were a better man than me, and a true friend.*

For the next year I wandered eastward, through Stockton, Carson City, Rawlins—places like that. I shoveled ore into carts, cut wheat, was a swamper in an eating house, herded cattle, broke horses. Never in all that time did I touch liquor, even though I tended bar for a while in Boise City. On a cold December morning I rode a spavined mare into Fort McPherson, the place I left with such hope and spirit seven years before.

The Indian Salvation School was empty, broken windows like eyeless sockets. Only a few companies of infantry occupied the post. The grounds were shabby and unkempt compared to the days when Fort McPherson had been a principal outpost for fighting the Sioux and the Cheyenne. At the wooden sheds along the river a sentry challenged me. When I told him I was Indian, and had people living there, he eyed me sourly and said, "You look like a white man. I can't say you resemble those brutes in there."

"The big difference between you and the brutes," I said, tying the mare, "is that you've got a gun and they haven't."

Ignoring his muttered oaths, I opened the door of the nearest shed and walked in. For a moment I drew back, sickened by the stench of unwashed bodies, sickness, tainted food. In that one small shed lived dozens of my people. Ragged and dirty, they huddled together for warmth. Some lay on straw pallets, others crouched in corners, gnawing at bones or picking lice from seams of their clothing. A single glass window was at the rear of the shed but did not give much light. Most of the panes were broken and stuffed with rags to keep out the cold. In the middle of the floor was a small iron stove with a few dying embers in it, no match for the December cold.

When I opened the door, no one looked up, no one seemed to care. It was like a winter nest of lizards, tangled together and squirming about, trying to keep life intact until some spring and the renewing sun.

On a rough wooden bench near the window sat an old man, face turned upward to catch a glimmer of the dying light. It was Doll Man, the *Tsistsista* cryer and father of Standing Alone.

"Honored old man," I said, "do you know me?"

As if expecting a blow, he drew back. His eyes were filmy and vacant-looking. "No," he mumbled, "I do not know you. Are you one of the soldiers who speaks our language?"

Who was I? The question baffled me. How should I answer?

When I did not respond, he turned his face again to the sun, a blind and helpless old man. Once he had yelled the news so loud it hurt your ears.

In an adjoining shed I found *Nish-Ki*, sick and feeble on a pile of dusty grain sacks. A strange woman bent over her, feeding her soup from a cracked pot. How old *Nish-Ki* had become! When I left she had been full of years but vigorous and hearty. Now she was thin and pale; the thick iron-gray hair was almost gone, only a few wisps straggling across her head. But it was *Nish-Ki*, and she knew me.

"Grandson!" she called. In spite of the woman's restraining arm, she struggled up, then fell back. "Look, everyone! Beaver Killer has come home!"

No one noticed. They thought the old woman was in a delirium, and went on playing the stick game on the dirt floor, squabbling among themselves over bits of bread they were betting.

"Yes," I said, "I am Beaver Killer, *Nish-Ki*. And I have come home."

She caught my hand, holding it to her cheek. "Little *Mok-so-is*," she crooned. "I am not dreaming."

For a long time I squatted there, letting her hold my hand. Then I realized the woman with the soup was looking at me, long and steadily. Finally she asked, "Do you know me, Beaver Killer?"

Slowly I raised my eyes. Before I saw the haggard cheeks, the signs of early ageing, I knew who she was. Standing Alone. For a long time we looked at each other like that. At last I said, "Yes. I know you."

Still holding my hand, *Nish-Ki* had fallen to sleep. Gently I pulled my hand from her grasp. Standing Alone laid down the cracked pot and tried to arrange her hair. "I have changed," she murmured. "Do not look at me, Beaver Killer. I am ashamed of the way I look."

"And I too," I said. "But that is the way it happened to us, you and me."

She drew me into a corner of the shed. From a recess among the loose boards she took a cloth-wrapped bundle. Saying no word of my vow, asking nothing about success or failure in my long absence, she handed me the *Mahuts*, the Sacred Arrows. "Your grandfather gave me these to keep for you," she said. "He knew some day you would come back. Now you are Keeper of the Arrows."

I was not worthy, certainly. But who else among these beaten people could be the Bearer of the Thunder Bow now, the Keeper of the Arrows?

As was my privilege, I unwrapped the bundle. There lay the *Mahuts*, straight and beautiful in my hands, matched shafts of finest red willow, points fashioned from deer antler. Remembering the Medicine Lodge ceremony so long ago, when I became *ho nuh ka wa*, the dedicated man, I stared curiously at them. Were they still there, the stains of dishonor the horse soldier Hazlitt had brought on the *Tsistsista*? It was dark in that corner, and I really could not tell. The shafts were dark and smoky-looking anyway, perhaps from long disuse and being hidden from the light.

"I thank you," I said to Standing Alone. Carefully I rewrapped the bundle. Arrows under my arm, I pulled her to me, pressing her cheek against mine. "Thank you again," I said, "for all you have done for *Nish-Ki*. You are a fine woman, and *Sweet Medicine* will someday reward you." I pointed to the *parfleche* cylinder hanging around my neck. "He sees everything, you know, and even though the life of the *Tsistsista* is now hard, everything will come out all right."

Outside it grew dark. A smoky orange sun hung over the Iron Mountains, where Grandfather had his big camp with so many lodges. The sour-faced sentry still walked his post, flapping his arms against the bearskin coat to keep warm.

"Soldier!" I called.

He slowed his pace. "What in hell do *you* want?"

"More coal for the stove in there," I told him. "The people are freezing."

He grinned as if I were an idiot. "Coal? That ain't any of *my* business! Talk to the quarter-master."

"All right, then," I said angrily. "Where do I find him?"

"Lieutenant Catlin," he said. "His office is over there by the flagpole."

Idiot? Maybe I was. I had been crazy for a long time. But I started off to see the quartermaster. Someone had to do it.

From a distance I looked back at the sprawl of unpainted sheds. I had come home; perhaps I had even fulfilled some small part of my vow. But I began to realize what I had paid for it. *Nish-Ki* was dying, Doll Man only a blind old man. Standing Alone stirred in me no emotion but pity. My people had lost all substance, like rich summer grass that dries and withers in the wind of autumn. The *Tsistsista*, my *Tsistsista*, were something to be read about in a book, a white man's book.

I did not want ever to go back into that stinking shed where the remnants of the *Tsistsista* now lived. I did not want to see again their poverty, their degradation. Instead, my mind filled with pictures; the shiny brass reading lamp in Mr. Barley's house in Salt Lake City, the great boats driving smokily up the Sacramento, Julie Hazlitt's pale face in the gloom of the conservatory of the house on the Clay Street hill.

The general had died, and so had I. If I had slain the devil horse soldier, I had slain Beaver Killer too. In my place was now a *siyuk*, a ghost; a perplexed and bewildered half-breed, a man not of that world nor of this. Only one small part of

Beaver Killer still remained; I was a dedicated man.

On the quartermaster's door was a wreath, green holly leaves sprinkled with red berries. A paper banner said *LORD JESUS LOVES YOU.* Resolutely I knocked on the door.